DEEP OVERSTOCK

#2: Fairy Tales, Fables, Folktales
July 2018

CH - FABLES/FAIRIES/FOLK

EDITORIAL

EDITORS-IN-CHIEF: Ariel Kusby & Mickey Collins

MANAGING EDITORS: Robert Eversmann & Piers Rippey

PROSE: Lee Bowman

POETRY: Ariel Kusby

ART: Piers Rippey

SOCIAL MEDIA: Ariel Kusby & Piers Rippey

WEB DESIGN: Robert Eversmann

INTERIOR DESIGN: Mickey Collins

COVER DESIGN: Oaktea

CONTACT: deepoverstock@gmail.com
deepoverstock.com

Letter from the Editors

Dear Readers,

Thank you for reading the second issue of Deep Overstock, the booksellers' journal.

Once upon a time (way back in March 2018), Deep Overstock started as a way to get booksellers connected and working creatively together. So many of our fellow bookstore employees are writers, illustrators, or comic artists. We wanted to give ourselves a deadline and a venue to explore new work.

With this issue, we hoped to draw in as many people as possible, and and is there a genre more universal than the fairy tale? As booksellers we come into contact with these stories every day. As kids we all grew up with them in one form or another. Who can forget stories about crowns that prick your finger and curse your family to generations of murder and cannibalism, or bewitchings because fairies in disguise watched you spit your gum on the street. (Just us?)

Our contributors have shown how many different directions we can take the fairy/folktale, from the very beginning, with a reimagined Eden, through shadow puppet theater and magic spells, to end with a happily (or not-so-happily) ever after.. Even Goldilocks herself would have to say that this issue is "just right."

We're also excited to announce the theme for our next issue: Paranormal Romance. We invite you to supernaturally seduce us ;)

Signed,

Deep Overstock Editors

The Shadow's Zoo of Shadows

by Jonathan van Belle

Alice found a white satin ring box, designed like a tiny treasure chest. She could not open the ring box, despite the serious effort she expended.

"Inside this box," murmured a newly appearing shadow, "is my shadow zoo. And it is beyond dazzling! Shadow-seahorses swimming shadow-seas, and shadow-silkworms spinning shadow-silk, and shadow-sparrows singing shadow-songs."

"All in this box?" Alice gave a puzzled look at the shadow on the cement floor.

"All in this box." The shadow echoed.

"But how?"

"One of your kind once said, 'I could be bounded in a nutshell, and count myself a king of infinite space.' That clementine-sized treasure chest is very much like a nutshell, and it can hold more than infinite space."

"How?"

There was a long silence.

"You might forget how to speak." The shadow began to ramble to itself. "You might forget that you never actually ever spoke. Would you know how to know anything without words? Without words, would you know that you do not know? Imagine having, from your very earliest moment, grown up locked in a little crawl space, or a closet, or a lightless room—like this cement room! No school, no conversation, nothing to read or hear, and no one."

"What about your shadow zoo?" Alice wanted desperately to do something kind and caring, and say something helpful.

"No one knows who I am, not even you." The shadow was dark on the cement. "Only dust. Floor and dust."

"I love your shadow zoo, I really do!"

But the shadow was unresponsive. It laid mutely on the cement, pulling its shadowy hair from its shadowy head.

Malin Kundang:
An Indonesian Folktale

by Sarah Nicole Donaldson

In a beachside village on the Island of Sumatra, there once lived a widowed mother and her son, Malin. Scarcely able to feed and clothe themselves, they suffered those regular indignities of folks in fairy tales whose poverty-stricken lives portend great rewards in the end.

A filial son, Malin cared for his mother as best he could. Every day at the crack of dawn, he'd walk to the village center where he sought work from the wealthiest villagers. These villagers, who'd never seen the bottoms of their rice barrels, paid him little more than a pittance to harvest their sugar cane or clamber up their coconut trees.

Malin worked until his arms and legs were scarred, and his cheeks stained with tears, all while his employers yelled at him to hurry up.

"Don't fall!" one of Malin's employers once told him, as the bamboo ladder teetered under his feet. "I don't want to pay someone to drag your rotting corpse out of my yard!"

On days he failed to procure any work, Malin offered part of his dinner to his mother, claiming his employers had fed him so well that he could hardly endure another spoonful of rice. At night, he chewed on billets of sugar cane to quiet his empty stomach.

"When I grow up," Malin often told his mother, "I'll save enough money to build you a grand house, bigger than any other on this island."

"Oh, but how will I manage to keep it clean?" the mother teased him.

"You won't have to do any housework. I'll hire ten servants to do all the cooking, washing, and cleaning. And every night we'll feast on beef curry and thousand layer cake."

"You say this now, but what will happen when you marry and have children of your own? You won't forget about your poor old mother, will you?"

"I'll never forget you," Malin said.

One day, a merchant ship arrived on the shore of their village. Malin, realizing this opportunity to build for himself a better life, asked for his mother's permission to work as a deck hand on the ship.

"Never again will we beg for food scraps," Malin promised her. "When I return, the beggars will come to our door and we will do some giving of our own!" They laughed at the absurdity of it.

Knowing she couldn't deny her son anything, the mother gave him her blessing. And so the ship set sail, with Malin in it, for foreign lands.

At every port the ship disembarked, Malin mailed a letter to his mother, in which he enclosed a generous portion of his wages. In these letters he told her of the wonderful adventures he'd had since the last letter, and how he wished that she too could share in his travels. True, the work was arduous, but each night he went to bed with a full stomach, and there wasn't much to complain about that.

Eventually Malin caught the attention of the ship owner, who praised him for his diligent work. Promoted to the position of third mate, Malin further proved himself to be an indispensible member of the crew. Tirelessly he worked through the ranks, until the day he was appointed as captain of the ship.

As in all great fairy tales, the ship owner offered Malin his daughter's hand in marriage, and they were wed in a most extravagant ceremony.

Meanwhile, Malin's letters grew fewer and farther between. The mother, ever trusting as she was, reasoned her son didn't have much time to write letters. He was a ship captain, after all, and a new husband besides.

And then there came the day the letters stopped.

When she had not a coin left in her coffer, the mother relied on her neighbors' pity to fill her dinner plate. "What an unfilial son you have," they told her, "to let his mother starve her way to the grave."

"My son hasn't forgotten about me," the mother said. "One day he will return to this village, and together we'll live in a grand house. He promised me this, himself."

The neighbors whispered among themselves that she was delusional, but what could they say? The woman couldn't be convinced that Malin had deserted her.

Many years later, Malin's ship did return to the village. Upon hearing the news, his mother went straight to the port to welcome him. Standing among the throng of villagers who'd come to see this poor boy-turned-captain, she breathed a sigh of contentment. How joyful she was, to see her handsome son standing beside his lovely wife, the two of them dressed in sumptuous silk clothing.

"See what I told you?" the mother said to her neighbors. "Today my son has come for me!"

The neighbors agreed that they were wrong about him.

"Malin!" the mother called to him. "It is I, your mother, come to bring you home."

As if she were a mosquito buzzing at his ear, Malin turned his head away.

"Malin!" she called, louder. "Perhaps you don't recognize me. It has been many years since I've looked upon your face. Come closer, my son, so I may—"

"Who are you, woman?" Malin asked her.

"Why, I'm your mother," she replied. "Surely you can see—"

"I have no mother," Malin said. "Certainly not one as dirty and poor as you."

Upon hearing these words, the mother wept bitterly. Forsaken by her only child, no physical blow could have stung her so.

What had become of the boy who sacrificed his youth to work the fields? The boy who shed his pride to fill his mother's dinner plate each night? This venerable man who stood before her, the mother thought, was not the son she raised.

"Malin," she said, wiping the tears from her eyes. "Is this how you speak to your mother? I, the woman who bore you, who nursed you of my breast, who cared for you—"

"Enough of your babble!" Malin said. "Get away from my sight, before I have you removed."

"What a fickle son you are!" the mother said. "Your heart is made of stone."

The moment those words fell from her lips, Malin's feet transformed to stone. "Wait!" Malin called after her, but she had already left for home.

To his wife, Malin said, "Hurry, my dear, for you must find my mother. Tell her to reverse this curse before it's too late." But when he reached for her hand, she recoiled from his touch. Lest she incur a similar fate, she fled from his side and ran aboard the ship.

Malin, did you forget your mother? Did you forget your promise to her?

Slowly the curse made its way up his legs, torso, arms, and neck, until only his head remained of flesh and blood. "Mother, help me!" he cried and cried, until the curse took hold of his tongue and he could cry no more.

Mermaid Bath Spell

by Ariel Kusby

Mermaids, mysterious and beautiful creatures of the deep, carry some of the most powerful magic on earth. Their beauty, intelligence, and special connection to the language of fishes and coral make them able to control the tides, creating the scariest tidal waves or the most serene snorkeling conditions. In this spell, you'll become a mermaid for awhile and harness the mighty powers of the sea.

Materials needed:
Bathtub
½ cup salt: (sea, epsom, or table)
A seashell
Optional: jewelry that won't tarnish, blue makeup

The spell:
Fill up your bathtub. Do whatever you can to feel most like a mermaid: let down your hair, put on some sparkly jewelry, or paint your eyes with shimmery blue makeup.

Sprinkle the salt into the bathtub, chanting: "Sea change, magical tides, make me a mermaid. Make me a watery spirit of the sea."

Slowly get into the tub, feeling the wetness caress your body like the gentle movement of waves at the sea bottom. Dip your head under the water so that your scalp gets completely wet, but you can still breathe. Feel your hair fan out or imagine it doing so, and let your body loosen and relax. Imagine that the tub is a bubble of sea foam from which you are being born.

Hold your shell to your heart, chanting, "Legs disappear, mighty tail emerge, dolphins and fishes guide me through the deep."

As long as you stay in the water, you will be a mermaid. What does it feel like have a tail, to move so gracefully through the water? Make friends with crabs and flounders, explore sunken shipwrecks, or experiment with creating storms.

When you're ready to get out, imagine that your legs re-appear like a magical sea creature who can transform into a human on dry land. As you climb out of the bath like a sea creature crawling out of the sea, remember that you can still be a mermaid on land if you want to be. It'll be your salty little secret.

A Troll's Soul
by Mickey Collins

Who knew that I'd be low below,

a troll 'neath a bridge,

waiting for my next toll,

gathering mold

eating stale rolls and making mountains out of mole

skulls

just wanting to haul

someone close to me

Knights often want to cross

those Sir Chads make me mad

but I'm a nice guy.

The name's Ross,

as I tip my hat

to the fair Ladies

The Knight sees this as a slight

and wishes to test his might

against my thick green skin

with a hope to win

the Lady's affection

by killing this infection

My skin can defend 'gainst swords

but not her words

as she cheers him on

even after he died

she's on his side

so below again I hide

I'll sometimes whisper dirty things so mean

they make her blush, make him squeam

but it never changes my poor fate

so I stew and become irate

And I cry, and wonder why why

why won't she consider a troll like me

(who's really a nice guy)

I'd buy her dresses and pour her tea

if she'd only get past my ugly

Once I tried to lure a maiden fair

down into my humble lair

by making pretend I was a knight

though my visage would give her a fright

so I hid behind a mask of steel

her heart I soon would steal

but she wasn't a fan of my piss bottles

or posters of anime models

and so she ran

And they all run on sight

but I spy up their skirts so I might

see something of interest

like peach or sweet citrus

if just a flash

as they pass

It's better this way

to be a creep in the deep

unlovable and unwanted

ugly and forgotten

a son misbegotten

the rats even hide from my smell

as others pass by my hell

unknowing and unflinching

uncaring

I'm not the only one here

I've got friends, other trolls

(all of 'em, nice guys)

a society of the deformed never to reform

cursed since being born

we ran from the scorn

but they're as bad at conversation as I

so it's pretty qui-

et

Below this bridge is our home

keeps us safe from the storms

though I can't help but feel more

that it's all something of a metaphor

The Stepfather's Dog

by Michael Calkins

There was once, outside the town of Waldheim, a man who had four dark-haired daughters. The daughters had no mother for she had died in giving birth to the youngest. The man bore the youngest no grudge for that and he did what he could to care for his four girls. He was not wealthy, but they always had enough to eat, warm beds in which to sleep, and sturdy clothes to wear.

There came a day, though, when the man began to feel that he would be happier, and his daughters would be better served, if he were to remarry. There was no eligible woman in Waldheim so he sent word to the neighboring towns and villages. After a time, a letter arrived at his home. There was a widow in Rotstadt who was looking to remarry now that she had ended her mourning period. The writer of the letter described her as a good, devout woman with a face like the full moon on a cloudless night. She was, also, the mother of a young boy named Johann.

The man kept this woman in mind for a number of weeks. When no other made herself known to him, he decided to contact the widow and invite her and her son to visit. Within the month, Johann and his mother found lodging in Waldheim. The widow's beauty did not, to the man's thinking, match the assertions of the letter writer, but she was a handsome woman and he found her pleasant company. Her son, though, he found too shy and quiet, though he was polite enough.

The man courted the woman for a socially acceptable period of time, then asked her to marry him. She agreed, of course, and soon enough they married. Over the next number of years they were happy together. The man had someone to oversee the household and help his daughters to become young women and his new wife had a stable home and a father for Johann, who slept in the barn because there was no room in the house for another bed.

As is the way of such things, however, Johann's mother became ill one day and, despite the loving care of her new family, she died. So much for her.

Johann grieved for his mother and also for himself, for he knew quite well that his stepfather did not like him. His stepfather had tempered his distaste for his stepson while Johann's mother had lived. But now he berated and belittled and beat the boy at every opportunity. Johann's stepsisters were sometimes sympathetic, especially the youngest who would sneak extra bites of cake out to the barn, but they could do little to protect their stepbrother.

One summer evening, Johann was sent to the barn without any dinner for no reason that the boy could recognize. Johann went to his bed and took a small bundle from beneath it. He clutched the sack to his chest and left the barn in the direction of the nearby woods. He did not go to town for he feared that someone would recognize him and return him to his stepfather. Soon enough he was too deep in the trees to see any part of his stepfather's property. In fact, it had become so dark beneath the canopy of leaves that he could barely see anything.

Johann reached into his sack for flint and steel and found them beneath the extra shirt and the bindle of bites of cake. Soon enough he had a fire burning. "You make the trees nervous with that," said a voice behind Johann, who jumped to his feet and nearly stumbled into the fire. He turned to the voice as he stepped around the fire to keep it between them.

A smallish man stood leaning against a tree. His hairless head fairly glowed in the light of the fire. Johann could not guess his age, for all adults, except the oldest, seemed of an age to him. The man sucked his teeth as he watched the boy. When it became obvious that Johann would not speak, the man said, "And you make me nervous with your silence. What is your name, boy?"

Johann took several breaths and swallowed once before saying, "My name is Johann."

"Humph! You can't spit these days without hitting a Johann. You're as common as fleas. Tell me, Johann, why are you setting my forest on fire?"

"I haven't!" He pointed at his little fire. "I've only burned some branches. For light. It became so dark here and I could not see where I was." Johann thought about running from the man, but his sack was on the other side of the fire and the woods were very dark not far from it. He decided to be as brave as he could.

The man stared at Johann. He said, "Tell me, what brings a boy out here alone to start conflagrations among my trees? What would your parents think?"

Johann decided that part of being brave was being honest and so he told the bald man the story of his stepfather's unkindness and the loss of his mother. He did so without tears, though he sometimes felt he might cry. This, also, seemed brave to him.

The man stood silently for a moment, scratching his chin, then said, "If you will agree to put out your fire, I will help you with your problem. I know a thing or two about fathers and sons." Johann looked at the fire and the darkness beyond it and the strange man. He knelt and grabbed handfuls of dirt to throw on the flames. Soon enough there was no light. And no sound from the man. Before Johann could do or say anything else, he fell asleep.

Johann woke to the sound of singing birds. He yawned and his long tongue curled up around the end of his nose. He stretched his legs, all four of them, and rolled onto his back to scratch it against the dirt. None of this seemed strange to him until he took a look at himself. He remembered being a boy and boys did not have paws or fur or tails, but he had all of these things now. He looked around for the bald man and called for him, but the sound he made was a deep, growling bark.

He barked again. He liked it. He stood and walked in circles until he felt he had always walked on all fours. The man was no-where to be seen or heard or smelled. Johann sat and thought, "I am a dog now." And, to his surprise, the thought was not un-pleasant. He sat and thought about being a dog until he began to feel hungry. Having no where else to go and no better idea of what to do, Johann decided to return to his stepfather's home.

He arrived to find his stepsisters busy outside with chores. As he approached, Johann called out to them. His barks sounded nothing like their names, but he had the girls' attention. They stopped their chores and watched the dog warily, as they should, for rabid animals were not unknown in the area. Johann sat. He wagged his tail and did his best to seem friendly.

The youngest girl was the first to approach. Her sisters cautioned her to be careful and held their axes and pitchforks ready. Johann sat quietly and when his stepsister began to scratch him between his ears he thought that nothing in his life had been better. His tail pounded the dirt. The other sisters joined the youngest and Johann was soon covered by petting hands and scratching fingers.

"What is this, then?" asked their father who had come from the house. The girls explained what had happened and asked, together, "Can we keep him?" Their father thought for a while and then agreed that they could, so long as no one came to claim the dog.

They ran around the yard with their new pet, throwing things for him to retrieve and laughing at his antics. Johann was happy to play in this way with his stepsisters. He fetched what they threw and accepted their hugs and kisses. "He will need a name," said their father who was happy to see his daughters happy.

Before the others could say anything, the youngest shouted, "Wolfgang!" Her sisters protested, for dogs named Wolfgang were as common as boys named Johann, but the deed was done. Johann became Wolfgang and was welcomed again to his new family.

Wolfgang slept in the barn as Johann had, but otherwise his life was better than before. He had no need to wear clothes or do chores. When he wanted to relieve himself, so long as he was not in the house, he could do so wherever he liked. And his stepfather seemed pleased with him now. The man would take Wolfgang into town to show him off to the men there, who were always impressed with how well-behaved and intelligent his dog was. For several years, such was Wolfgang's life.

There came a day when Wolfgang, pleasantly tired from an afternoon of chasing rabbits, returned to the barn for a nap. All four of his stepsisters were there talking about something. Wolfgang sat next to the youngest, who could be relied on for the best back scratching. The eldest sister was speaking.

"Father has decided, I tell you. We're all to be married next spring. I overheard him talking in town. He has promised the butcher, the barber, the undertaker and the pig farmer our hands in marriage." There were cries of protest from the others. They found fault with all the men, who were too old, too smelly, too fat, or too lacking in teeth, among other faults. The sisters wanted nothing to do with any of them. The eldest assured her sisters that their father would not be dissuaded from these matches for his position in town would be much improved when they were made.

Wolfgang had only partly been paying attention when the youngest became so animated in her objections that she stopped scratching his back. He decided to retire to his corner to sleep when Wolfgang heard the eldest sister tell the others her plan. How, tomorrow, on the anniversary of their mother's death, when their father was known to drink too much and pass out in his bed, they would use their knives and axes to end his life, and their marriage problems.

Her sisters were silent for a long while, giving her plan due consideration, but, finally, they agreed it was the only sensible thing to do. Wolfgang growled low before knowing what he was doing. "What about Wolfgang?" asked the second sister. "He's very loyal to Father. He might get in the way." The sisters agreed that they would tie Wolfgang in the barn earlier that day to keep him from causing mischief. When they were satisfied with the particulars of their plan they went into the house to make dinner.

Wolfgang paced across the barn. His mind was a confusion of ideas. He did not want to believe what he had heard his sisters planning. He chased some chickens to clear his mind, then found himself running from his stepfather's barn toward Waldheim.

Wolfgang ran first to the butcher's shop. He barked and yowled until the butcher came to the door. The man threw some offal in the dirt for the dog. "Where is your master today, boy?" he asked. Wolfgang yipped and turned in circles but could not make the man understand. The butcher watched the dog for a while then went back into his shop. Wolfgang looked at the closed door in disappointment then turned toward the barber's shop, then turned back to the offal and ate it all before being off again.

The barber's door was open and Wolfgang went inside where he was greeted cheerfully by the barber and his customers. Wolfgang huffed and shook and clawed the floor, but he was no better understood here than at the butcher's. Soon enough the men grew tired of his antics and one of them escorted Wolfgang outside and shut the door behind him. The undertaker was no more insightful and the pig farmer became angry at Wolfgang for scaring his sows and chased the dog away.

On his way back to the barn, his head hanging, Wolfgang passed the woods where he had met the bald man. He sat and looked in among the trees. There was no sign of the man. Still, Wolfgang made up his mind and walked into the darkening wood. When he came to the place where he had last been a boy named Johann, he howled and barked and growled, hoping to attract the bald man's attention. He did this for a long time and when it seemed obvious that no one would come, Wolfgang lay in the fallen leaves and fell asleep.

When he woke birds were singing. Wolfgang yawned and his long tongue curled out over his nose. The bald man had not come, obviously, for the dog was yet a dog. He stood and looked toward his home. If his stepfather was to be saved, then, Wolfgang knew, his dog would have to do it.

Wolfgang waited at the edge of the property among the bushes, where his stepsisters would not see him. He kept an eye on them through the day as they went about their chores. No one who had not been in the barn with them could possibly tell what they had in mind as they milked and chopped and laughed as usual. In the late afternoon, when Wolfgang knew that his stepfather would be well into his cups, all four sisters went into the barn.

He padded to the door of the barn and listened. The girls were talking of girlish and sisterly things without a hint of murder. They did this for so long that Wolfgang began to hope that their plans would come to nothing, that they had changed their minds during the night. Then he heard the eldest ask the others if they preferred the knife, ax, cleaver, or pitchfork. Wolfgang, remembering his last moments as Johann, decided to be brave again and ran into the barn.

The dog barked and growled and bared his fangs at his stepsisters who each held something sharp. They shouted and screamed at the bristling animal. "He's gone mad," said the third sister. They scurried back to protect themselves as Wolfgang snapped his jaws in the direction of each. Only the youngest had stood her ground and had reached for the dog. Wolfgang stopped his snapping and barking suddenly. Something unexpected was in his mouth.

He felt the blood spurting from his youngest stepsister's wrist. The second sister grabbed her sibling's wounded arm and pulled her back as the first and third charged the vicious animal. The pitchfork's tines and the cleaver's blade had done their work before Wolfgang could spit out the severed hand. He collapsed to the straw and died.

The sisters surrounded the youngest. They bound the wound as best they knew how and did what they could to soothe her. They sat quietly together for a time. The eldest, not wanting to let a good plan go to waste, told the third sister to follow her and bring her chosen weapon. They went to the house and found their father as drunk and unconscious as they had hoped. It was no time at all before he followed Wolfgang into death. The sisters worked quickly to drop their father into the dry well that he had meant to fill someday. They filled it just enough to hide his body. So much for him.

Soon enough they were in Waldheim having the youngest sister's wound tended and telling the story of a father who had gone mad and attacked his daughters, raving nonsense and siccing his dog on the girls. And how the dog had bitten off the hand of the dearest young one and the mad father had come to his senses enough to run away. And how the girls had found enough courage to kill the vicious dog.

Everyone believed the girls, of course. For after some of the men visited the farm, they found that the father was, indeed, gone and the dog was, undeniably, dead. So much for him. And, of course, the youngest girl was without her right hand, which lay on the floor of the barn. There was great sympathy for them and many offers to help. The sisters accepted some of the help, but they turned aside all offers to sell the farm or to come stay with them to help work it. They turned aside, also, all offers of marriage. The four suitors their father had found for them pursued the sisters for a time. But one by one the men became discouraged and stopped calling at the farm.

Over the years, as they went to town less and less, the sisters became a curiosity to the townspeople who would tell stories about the spinster sisters and their brush with death. This did not bother the sisters one bit and they lived long, happy lives together. The youngest never bore Wolfgang a grudge for what he had done, for she believed he had bravely defended his master at the cost of his own life. And when she died, no more than six months after her sisters, she was glad that she had once had such a dog. So much for her. So much for them.

So much for this.

RaPUNzel

by Dan Heise

Once a pun a time,
In a kingdom far away,
There lived a king and queen,
And their daughter, or so they say.

This daughter, the princess,
Was of unparalleled beauty.
Gorgeous, beautiful, ravishing,
Indeed, she was a cutie.

But not only that, she was smart too,
Reading everything in sight,
She took in info like a sponge,
Trying to learn everything just right.

Eventually, the princess came of age,
Much to the king and queen's delight.
Right then they started to plan and plot
About Rapunzel's wedding night.

"She's beautiful and smart," they said,
"And not the least bit sleazy.
What man wouldn't want to have her?
Marrying her off should be easy!"

But as they sent princes to her,
That's when the trouble began,
For no one could ever handle,
Of what Rapunzel was a fan.

For the princess liked to joke a lot,
Causing groans to all who heard,
For Rapunzel liked nothing more
Than a clever play on words.

"Just stop, we beg you!"
The king and queen would scream,
"You must be married! No man will take you!

To be married should be your dream!”

But Rapunzel would simply shrug,
“I need someone who won’t run.
One day someone will enjoy my words,
Then I’ll know I’ve found the pun.”

One day there came a prince,
Gallant, bright, and rich,
He strode up to the castle,
Ready to make his pitch.

“I’ve heard of Rapunzel,”
He said, “and her brand of fun.
Don’t worry, I can take it,
I can handle a simple pun.”

“You don’t understand,” said the King and Queen,
“For Rapunzel goes for quantity over quality!
The prince merely shrugged and said,
“How bad can it possibly be?”

The prince moseyed through the castle,
Having their warnings ignored,
And gleefully he arrived
At Rapunzel’s bedroom door.

He knocked, the door opened,
And the prince had the privilege
Of seeing for the first time
Rapunzel’s stunning visage.

“Rapunzel,” he stammered,
Embarrassed now and nervous,
“I’m the prince, come for your hand,
To be forever at your service.”

“I’m glad you have met me at this happy time,”
Said Rapunzel with a bow,
“I used to be in trouble and addicted to soap,
But don’t worry, I’m clean now.”

The prince suppressed the anger

That was climbing up his throat,
He nodded at her politely;
She wouldn't get his goat.

Making small talk, he said,
"Do you have to clean your own room?
Sorry I was looking around
And noticed that you have a broom."

Rapunzel smiled shyly, saying,
"I suppose I must offer an explanation.
I just had to try this broom out myself;
They say it's sweeping the nation."

The prince inhaled sharply,
His knuckles turning white,
He just had to make it now,
She'd be his before the night.

Rapunzel saw she had him on the ropes,
It was time to foil the plot.
To make him leave, she decided,
She'd hit him with her best shot:

"I submitted ten puns to a contest,
Right before it ended,
And when I looked to see which one won,
Sadly, no pun in ten did."

The prince blinked once stupidly,
Stunned by the awful comedienne.
He spun on a heel, walked out the door,
And was never seen again.

Again and again this happened,
Princes came and went,
Eventually, none were left,
All of their patience had been spent.

The king and queen threw up their hands,
Beating their hands and feet,
"We can't do it! We'll find no one!
The Princess drives away every man she meets!"

Suddenly, a prince appeared,
He came from a faraway land,
With him came a friend of his,
Each talking with their hands.

The king and queen looked on confused,
Wondering, "What was this?"
Who were these people? What were they doing?
Is there something that we missed?"

The prince made a gesture,
And the friend replied, "Yes, yes."
Turning to the king and queen he said,
"The prince wants to marry the princess."

"Right," said the king
Clearly not believing,
"But what's with all the gesturing?
What's with all the hand waving?"

"Ah," said the friend, "Of course,
I apologize most sincerely,
But the prince was born afflicted,
And cannot hear so clearly.

"Still, all he asks for is a chance,
Please don't turn him down,
He's smart, funny, capable,
Overall, the best around."

The king and queen couldn't believe their luck,
Finally, an end to all their fear.
For standing right before them
Was a prince who could not hear!

"This is perfect!" they rejoiced,
"Everything will be ok!
He can't hear, she'll get tired of saying them,
And finally the puns will go away!"

They ushered him into Rapunzel's room,
And told her before they left,
"You're all done now Rapunzel!

How will you pun to someone already deaf?"

But Rapunzel flashed a sly grin,
She's been busy with her time.
For while alone in her spare moments,
She had learned to sign!

She stood to greet the prince,
And then her hands they flew,
Signing, "Talking with your hands?
I've gotta HAND that to you!"

But then the prince grinned widely back,
He knew he had found the one,
He signed back in a happy flurry,
"You know, I've always loved to pun."

Then the two lived happily ever after,
These two joyous wordsmiths.
And now we draw our tale to a close,
This one's pun and over with.

Bobbi the Mermaid
by Kellye McBride

Bobbi, with an "i", was staying with the Pryces, who owned a fish restaurant. They said she could sleep in the lobster tank, which was uncomfortable but at least it was full of seawater. Bobbi's tail kept splashing, scaring the lobsters who scuttled to the other side.

"Do you think we should get a bigger one?" said Miriam Pryce to her husband, Hal, one night. Hal grunted.

"A bigger what?"

"A bigger tank. So Bobbi could be more comfortable."

Hal's nostrils quietly whistled and he said nothing until Miriam poked him a second time. "I s'pose," he replied finally, before drifting off to sleep.

Bobbi's presence in the tank unnerved the customers. At first, they thought it was some kind of publicity stunt, but Hal and Miriam went on KATU and assured the general public that Bobbi was, indeed, a real live mermaid. She was an exchange student from Atlantis. When Hal and Miriam retired and their children moved out, it got lonely in their little two-bedroom house on the East Side, that Hal's parents bought in the 1930s. So, they applied to a program that placed foreigners with American families wanting to learn English. Only when Bobbi showed up in an airtight crate filled with seawater did they realize that they should have been a little more specific with the paperwork. Housing a mermaid wasn't exactly easy.

Bobbi only spoke a few words in English, she spoke mostly Mermish or whatever they speak down in Atlantis. Mermish had a guttural sound to it, like the bark of a sea lion. From what Miriam gathered from the wet documents pinned to the crate, back home, Bobbi was failing English and needed to learn enough so she could graduate from Mermaid School and attend college. There was a separate attached list of food allergies attached, but the ink on the page had blurred, so Miriam had

no idea what it said. She could guess though. Miriam offered
Bobbi a sandwich once and Bobbi screamed so loud the gills on
the sides of her neck puffed out, so Miriam put "sandwiches"
on the new list. Bobbi only seemed to eat raw fish, which was
fine, there was plenty of it. She liked the fish heads that the
cooks usually threw out, so Miriam just had them save them in
a bucket for Bobbi.

Soon, small crowds came to the restaurant to ogle Bobbi.
Miriam wasn't sure how Bobbi was handling the attention, but
Hal thought that she seemed to be doing just fine. Bobbi would
scream something in Mermish and splash her tail around,
and the locals snapped photos and demanded selfies with her.
Bobbi's gender was something of an enigma, because Hal and
Miriam mistakenly assumed that all mermaids were women.
There were two small lumps of fat on her chest that indicated
breasts, but they were covered in scales. Bobbi had long, flow-
ing blue hair, but there was also some stubble on the sides of
her chin. Bobbi seemed to favor the good-looking busboys who
fed her lunch from a bucket, but she also liked the pretty young
women who took endless pictures of her. Miriam thought that
Bobbi was just being friendly, but then Bobbi's gills became
all red and engorged the same way they had with the busboys,
and she had to quietly ask the young women to leave. "I guess
it doesn't matter," Hal finally said at the dinner table one night
after a long debate about whether Bobbi was a girl or not.

Bobbi also started to steal things. At first it was harmless stuff,
like tiny bags of oyster crackers that were served with clam
chowder or butter pats. But over time Bobbi starting felching
things from the customers that posed for a photo op: jewelry,
rolls of film, sunglasses, baseball caps. Anything that was not
securely fastened on the customer's person tended to end up in
the bottom of the lobster tank, only to be fished out by a very
annoyed Hal who offered the customers a voucher for free clam
chowder. It got out of hand very quickly when Bobbi grabbed
a woman's service dog and tried to drown it, both of them
screaming and thrashing in the tank. The very wet and startled
Pekingese was returned to the woman, and Hal and Miriam had
to close down the restaurant for the afternoon because the other
guests became uncomfortable and left.

"What are we going to do?" Miriam said to Hal when all the restaurant was empty and Bobbi quietly returned to her normal splashing and babbling in Mermish. Hal had an idea, but he decided that he should wait until nightfall. He filled a cooler that he and Miriam sometimes took on camping trips with as much seawater as he could, and with the help of one of the cooks, stuffed Bobbi inside. Bobbi screamed from inside the cooler, and Hal and the cook wrapped bungee cords around it to be sure that it stayed closed. Once they carried the cooler out to Hal's truck, Hal tipped the cook handsomely and started to drive. He got on Highway 26 en route to Astoria and Cannon Beach, the quickest way to the ocean from Portland. He turned on the local country music station as loud as he could to muffle Bobbi's screams from the covered bed of the truck.

When they finally reached the coast, they were bathed in moonlight. He opened the back and tugged on the bungee cords, pulling the cooler out of the truck until it fell onto the beach. He dragged the cooler toward the waves, and then, with his pocketknife, severed the bungee cords, causing Bobbi to spill out onto the surf. Bobbi's long body unfurled in the waves, scales glossy and smooth. She flexed her tail, and then in one swift motion, dove into the tide and disappeared. She never resurfaced, and Hal thought good riddance as he drove back to the city, mermaid-less. Miriam was waiting for them on the steps outside their house, waving him down as he drove into their covered garage.

"You have to turn back," she said breathlessly.

Hal looked at her confused. "I thought you wanted her to leave."

Miriam shook her head, blinking back tears. "I found her diary while you were gone."

Sure enough, Miriam had. Bobbi had stolen a notebook from the front desk near the lobster tank which she filled with calligraphy, drawings of the Pryces, and poems about the various customers she liked. There were some very crude passages in English too, about how grateful she was staying in her new home and how much she loved her new human family.

"We can't just leave her out there in the open ocean, all alone," said Miriam.

Hal looked up at the moon and sighed. "All right. Let's go find her."

Late Night Pomes: Fairy Tales

by bb, Mickey Collins, Joe Galván, Sara Kachelman, Ariel Kusby, Olivia Olivia, Phoenix Singer, Piers Rippey, Robert Torres, Katie Borak, and Andy Anderson

Dear travelers of the deep, dark woods,

We see you have a basket of breads and beautiful chocolates. We see you are nice in your heart and mean to do well by your grandma. But the trees are made of glass and there is an old soldier inside one. Be careful, friend.

Write a line about a character in a fairy tale setting. Pass to the left, continue the story.

Every Last One of Them

Armed with nothing but a big fork, I left the family farm.

My friend the talking cat meowed. She carried the matching spoon.

A healthy snack: an apple filled with absinthe.

Godmother beckons to me: Grab the knife out of my ass and I will grant you three wishes.

I took the knife and fork. I ate everyone. But it tasted like straw smells.

Desperately Well-Known

Have you ever walked into a village of strangers who all somehow know your name?

Everyone is burning an effigy of you and the effigy is a bloody rose.

I lost a friend. How could they all tell? They came up behind me, asking me what happened.

I struck them all with rosewater and the city bloomed axes, first through their skulls, then in their limbs, then thin slices.

The city is named after me now and I am the only one inside it.

Tommy

Tommy (MADE OF LEATHER) trapped in a cave full of balloons.

Every night he dreamt that he had hands made of sewing needles.

Gold thread laced in pleather adorned his machine.

He woke up, still made of leather.

But no longer in a cave, nor a room, nor a tower, no, now squeaky safe in the arms of a lover.

George the Conversationalist

George, the world's finest auto-mechanic is trapped in the world's most boring conversation.

The wheel doesn't turn.

It was his fault to start.

But it took two to tango, and George dropped his amateur dancing partner and her small talk.

Silence.

Words took her over again, as he bandaged her knees.

The Littlest Insomniac

The little boy's scabs opened bloody on the factory floor, his fingers barely holding on attempting to work the spindle.

The shift manager (also a white-haired witch) asked, Would he like to go to sleep forever?

Skinned knees, skinned fingers, and undone conscience the little boy didn't cry but told his manager, Yes.

Still sleep wasn't an option for the young insomniac.

He sat and stared as the wall turned white.

The god in his rompered-wisdom held up a hand and proclaimed, "CHAOS!"

Dear travelers deep into magical realms,

We love what you've given us. In our soft hands. Your heart, here represented by a glowing sewing needle.

Bestow a 'magical object' to the poet on your right. The magical object should be significant to you. You are potentially saving a friend with it. Write a fairy tale, line by line, passing the paper to the right.

Two Castles

Timbo is in a glass castle surrounded by a moat of really hot asphalt.

Timbo has a love-of-his-life trapped in a very nearby castle made of steel.

They can only communicate via tin-can phones, the kind held together by a taut string.

They talk about the storms.

Timbo says into the can, "I love you."

Timbo's love says back, "No."

Big Hole

She hollered, "Help! I am stuck in a big hole!"

"It's the biggest hole I've ever laid my eyes on," he said.

"It is whispering sweetly something about me," she said.

"I wish I knew what it was whispering. I don't speak 'Big Hole.'"

"I only speak Black Hole."

Sunken Ship

Sebastien is trapped in a cab sunken like a ship.

Bombed thrice, enough…

"Four is too many, two is too little," said Sebastien.

"All the skeletons were blown apart like far-reaching explorers.

And their hopeful widows watched the horizons for their lost loves, forever more."

Dear friends of Little Hans,

We are worried for Little Hans.

Write the first word you think of, on a small piece of paper, when I say … "Married Object" … then pass this small written object to the left. There is still warmth in my hands. Please unfold your object. Realize it was the only thing that ever mattered to Little Hans. But now somebody will take it away. That someone is you…

Pass back and forth between your many hands. You are the kind ruiners of Little Hans' fate. How did he lose his fate?

I Only Wanted Eyes

Little Hans had no signal.

He wanted your eyeballs.

Your brittle hands were too weak

to stop him from prying open your lids.

Salt and Pepper Might Go Together but Rivers Washed My Love Away

Little Hans wanted pepper but instead got a river.

The river was the world's only salt producer.

It wasn't a river; it was an ocean!

Little Hans was so scared of all the massive potential.

My Mother and the Bees Both

Little Hans had a bouquet to obtain bees.

They swarmed slowly, trickling into his hollow

Little Hans led his little bees to his mother's home.

His mother was allergic and thought that birthing Hans was a very bad deal.

Little Hans mined out a diamond.

Little Hans held it in the pocket of his heart,

an excavation tool.

He had no heart left.

Dear weary travelers,

We are all worried we are not created by something special, are we not? Are we worried we are not bewitched or cursed? Are we older than we look? We are afraid. We need answers.

Receive an object. Consider this object the spark of creation for an image of someone lodged into your heart, as if lodged into an egg, the egg into the stomach of the goose, the stomach in the pouch of a marsupial, and the marsupial in an ancient, crying tree. These are our creation myths.

Pink Sword

The pop star in a pink dress, with a sequin sword—from her lips, a duet began.

No Diamonds Left

In a land devoid of diamonds or precious gems, the people gave each other objects of immense beauty to ask for marriage. A young man to woo his lover, sculpted the most beautiful tale he could imagine to give his lover an object of perfect beauty. His lover was so infatuated they washed that face would come to life.

Bubble Boy

In the beginning, the world was water. And then it began to boil. Hot steamy bubbles. One bubble emerged and a young boy popped out. The young boy fell to his knees on the beach. He saw the sky, the mountains, the rivers, the city, all for the first time. The boy wept. For he was never meant to leave the ocean.

Grey Leg

She was born in the leg of a great grey giant. She called upon the spiders to come and cut her out. She crawled up the giant, her father, shipwreck still and unwatching, to see his chest was full of holes. The holes were shaped like her. They had arms and heads and legs. She climbed into one, but immediately fresh hands shoved her out. She crawled up her father's chest toward a higher hole, another one just like her. It too pushed her away. It seemed there were no holes left for her to crawl into. Every one shoved her away. She crawled down her father and wandered the barren earth.

Parthenia

by Joe Galván

Once upon a time, there was a man who lived in a tower at the edge of the world, in the kingdom of Highcliff. In his youth, he had been wise enough to reject the meaningless things of this world, and at the age of thirty, left the court of nobility with his young wife, a lady of simple beauty and elegance. Resolving themselves to retire from the world and its noise, they built a house at the edge of the ocean, far away from any other man, and before heaven and earth, swore to live a life of peace and quiet.

Very soon the man and his wife had a child, a baby girl whom they named for a famous Siren, for when she was born, she emerged from her mother's womb with the sweetest cry they had ever heard. And so, the man, being eminently well-disposed in his knowledge of Greek myth, named the girl Parthenope, for this Siren, it was said, not only wooed the young Odysseus on his way back to Ithaca with her sweet voice, but also could charm the waters of the sea and the four winds to abet the will of the gods themselves.

The man and his wife and child lived in harmony at the edge of the sea. Their lives were as halcyon as could be, and each warm afternoon, all three would run down to the shore and collect the treasures that the sea deposited there. The man would fish, and his wife and his child would gather shells and gems on the beach. The man would collect crabs and lobster and clams and all kinds of delicious and flavorful fish, and cook them on the shore, and would tell them stories of the heroes of the ancient past, and the saints who had braved the waves and the winds to travel to distant lands.

One day, some awful affair in the city of Holywood required that the King request this man's assistance, and he sent a page on a white horse with a white banner to the kingdom of Highcliff. In the city of Holywood there had been much intrigue, for the Queen had taken ill and consulted a witch to make her fair and young again. But instead of making her beautiful and fruitful enough to bear the King a first-born son, the medicine that this witch had made instead made the Queen so ugly and undesirable that any mirror she stood in front of broke, and all the people (even her attendants and ladies-in-waiting), and even the King, was utterly repulsed by her. When the page arrived at Highcliff, a storm was about to break over the sea. The man, sensing the urgency of the King's request, went straight away, leaving his wife and their daughter in the fortified tower. The man took a ship to the city of Holywood, which lay on an island across the sea.

That night there was a storm not seen before or since. The waves broke on the highest rocks and pounded against the immense cliff. The sea was much disturbed, and the clouds raced across the sky in all directions; the gales tore branches from the trees and the waves dashed anything loose against the shore. This storm lasted seven days and seven nights. The woman took her daughter down to the cellar of the tower to keep her safe, and there read to her by candlelight the life of St Barbara, who had once been imprisoned in a high tower for her faith.

At midnight on the seventh night the woman emerged on the parapet of the tower just as the storm was breaking for a moment, and through the moonlight she saw her husband's coracle hovering on the waters, with his marvelous lantern that no water could extinguish burning brightly from the mast. Indeed, the man had returned from Holywood, having cured the Queen of the scrofulous malady inflicted on her by that malefic agent of Satan himself, the witch. With him he bought a bag of gold as payment from the King himself.

But as she rejoiced at her husband's return—lo! The storm renewed its violence, and with an immense wave swept the woman from the parapet of the tower to her doom below. The man saw it all happen from his coracle, and sped home against the wind and waves and arrived on the yellow sands, his ship and his spirit broken.

The man buried his wife in a cave with the lantern whose lamp never went out and resolved to mourn for her for the rest of his life. Now that he was a widower, he swore to spend all of his time studying forbidden knowledge, utterly embittered that God Himself could be so cruel. In time, this bitterness abated somewhat, and he instead focused all his attention on rearing his daughter to be as beautiful and as graceful as his wife had been.

First, he taught her to sing. He roused her with porridge at breakfast and taught her the scales on a flute fashioned from a whale bone. Next, he taught her melody and rhythm, by teaching her the cadence of the waves and the song of the sea birds. He taught her to read and write, until she could speak her own tongue and Latin and Greek and write in all the same. Then, he instilled knowledge of sacred harmony and the rites that attended it, so that in time, she could be awakened by the very music of the spheres themselves, which only he could hear.

But in return for all these things, he forbade her expressly to leave the tower, and most certainly to marry. And to make this so, he fashioned for her from sacred wood gathered from the four points of the earth, a marvelous instrument. He enchanted it and wrote music for her, inscribing the notes in gold on parchment. Both book and instrument were enchanted so that it could never be drenched by water nor scorched by flame. The man fashioned this harpsichord, which he called Parthenia, in just seven days' time, and by the evening of the eighth day, she was playing it for him while he warmed his hands at the fire.

For many years it was like this, until Parthenope grew into a young woman, blessed by God with beauty and grace, the most beautiful woman who had ever existed in that part of the world. No man other than her father had seen her, but her renown grew as sailors' tales of her singing and playing reached the kingdoms of Holywood, Fairmount, Fountainvale and Flower-field.

It so happened one fine summer day that the Prince of Fair-mount, returning from fighting the heathens in the lands across the sea, passed by the coast on which Parthenope lived. Parthe-nope had been accompanying herself on the magical harpsi-chord. Dropping anchor just off the coast, he and his page embarked in a small dinghy and made their way toward the shore.

Parthenope, on first apprehending the sight of the Prince of Fairmount, had never seen such a beautiful man as he. His hair was chestnut like the robur oaks of the forest, his beard was handsomely clipped close to his chiseled face, and his eyes were like two shining emeralds set in a bowl of milk. He had the form of a man of nobility, but he was more athlete than limp wristed nobleman. She could see he had spent many days on the sea, as was more a fisherman than a prince.

Once the prince was onshore, he looked up at the immense crooked tower that arose from the yellow cliffs overlooking the sea.

'Hello up there!' The Prince said.

The wise man saw all this happen and ran up to his daughter, who had been combing her hair at the window.

'Someone is ashore,' the man said to Parthenope. 'Don't you dare stir from this room.' And he locked the door and went downstairs.

'What do you want?' The wise man cried from behind an iron gate.

'I heard some beautiful music from the sea, as I was passing in my ship here, and could not bear another moment not knowing whom or what it was.'

'It was the wind, my friend! The wind and nothing more,' the old man replied.

The prince stood there, incredulous that this old man would tell him—a man of the world—that the sound he had heard emerging from the coast was naught but the sound of the wind.

'Pray tell me, old man, did you not hear that marvelous young woman singing of the waves and the sea, of the sea foam that falls on the rocks? Could you not hear what I heard?'

'I must confess, I heard nothing, my lord,' the old man replied.

The prince drew his sword and advanced toward the old man behind the grille.

'I know what I heard. Who is it that you have locked in this tower? I can see that you are evidently a most powerful wizard, and in Christ's name, I will cut off your hands and suspend them from your stole if you don't tell me whom you're holding up there in that tower.'

'My daughter,' the old man replied. 'And there's no way you can get to her. I've locked the door and she can't come out to you.'

The Prince of Fairmount looked up towards the beautiful Parthenope, sitting at her window. She had been playing her harpsichord and singing. The music was beautiful and sumptuous. He had never heard anything like it before.

'I will give you as much gold as you will have for that woman's hand in marriage. I am the Prince of the Kingdom of Fairmount, a man renowned in the heat of battle. I am ready to give you as much as you want for her. If you are her father, I will give you anything for her dowry. I can make you a very, very wealthy man.'

'I wouldn't give her up for all the gold in the world, for she is my only happiness. And I would rather curse her and you for all time with misfortune and unhappiness than give her up.'

The Prince, steeled in his resolve, struck the lock off the iron grille that separated him from the tower grounds.

'I am not to be refused,' the Prince replied. 'Bring her down, and I'll spare your life.'

The old man, already wise enough to expect this sort of response, went up to her room and said to her calmly, 'My daughter, the Prince of Fairmount has asked me for your hand and I have refused. He has asked me once more and I have refused again. Now he has asked me a third time, and as the custom of our country ordains, I have no choice but to give you away to him.'

'Father, I will not depart from you,' Parthenope said.

'I will give you up,' he replied. 'The Prince has promised me all the gold and gems in the world for you, but you are more precious than that. Therefore, go, daughter, pack up your clothing and all your finery, and go with him, but do not endeavor to look on my face or call my name again, for in the day that you do, you will most surely die.'

'Father, what will become of you?'

The old man did not respond to this question, but instead went to the harpsichord that sat before the window looking out at the shore.

'You see this fine instrument that I made you to entertain me in my grief. Now it will be the very thing that binds you to your fate. For in the day that you cease to play this instrument for any reason, even for bearing a son, you will be stricken with ugliness and no man will want you.'

Horrified at this prospect, Parthenope asked, 'Why, my father, after all this time in which I have loved you and lived only for you, why would you do such a thing to me? Have I not attended to you? Have I not resolved to die for you? I would rather die a thousand deaths than to be married over to that man down below, if such a union pains you so.'

But the wise old man knew what was to happen. 'His page,' he replied, 'will fetch your things, and you will depart from here as soon as there is a fine wind to take you. Today is the last day you will ever set eyes on me.'

The wise old man brought out his daughter at last and gave her hand to the Prince of Fairmount.

'You see what your lack of compromise has gotten you,' the old man said. 'I will give my daughter to you, but in the day that she ceases to play her beloved harpsichord, she will become as ugly and as useless to you as the barnacles on the underside of your ship, and she will join them in the depths of the ocean.'

The Prince of Fairmount smirked and said, 'She will be my

Queen, and your curses and threats will dissolve like smoke in the air. You did not tell me how beautiful your daughter is. Your hair, my lady, is more beautiful than spun gold, and your eyes are like two sapphires. You will have no use of musical instruments. In my kingdom, only courtesans play the harpsichord. You shall have at your disposal a whole orchestra to play for you any time you wish.'

'My lord, I humbly beg your forgiveness,' Parthenope replied, 'but I cannot live without my harpsichord. I beg you, be kind to me and let me take it with me to your kingdom.'

Reluctantly, the Prince agreed and allowed Parthenope to take her beloved harpsichord with her. Two of the Prince's slaves brought down the harpsichord that very day and brought it back to the Prince's ship. Her father turned his back on her as they were leaving, and she could not help but weep thinking she was never to see her father again.

On the Prince's ship, the Prince introduced Parthenope to the crew and commanded they make obeisance to their new queen. He moved her in to his quarters and immediately set sail for the Kingdom of Fairmount.

Parthenope and the Prince of Fairmount were married, and all was well for a little while. The King of Fairmount gave her a magnificent crown of diamonds and sapphires, and an emerald dress more splendid that any dress ever seen in the kingdom. The Prince ordered for her baths of rose petals and donkey milk to make her skin even more soft and supple than it already was. He also gave her the largest and most sumptuous chambers in the palace and entrusted twelve ladies-in-waiting to attend to her every desire.

While she was kind and courteous, inside Parthenope was languishing, and what was more, afraid of her future. She could not play music, nor could she sing, for singing and the playing of instruments in the Kingdom of Fairmount was a shameful thing, something that worldly courtesans and the low-born women of the street did. When Parthenope sang it was at chapel early in the morning, when only her confessor could hear her.

The King had begun to serenade her beneath her window in the dead of the night, as was the custom in Fairmount among young men in love. Parthenope, aware of the tradition, knew that once he had serenaded her twice an answer was expected—and he already serenaded her once. She was expected in little time to bear him an heir.

At night, Parthenope could not sleep, for even the very idea of some awful curse hanging over her was enough to keep her up at night. Very soon, she became anxious to inquire on the whereabouts of her harpsichord.

One night she asked a guard to come into her presence immediately.

'I command you, in the name of this fair kingdom, to tell me where my harpsichord is.'

The guard wavered and said the Prince had, upon his marriage to Parthenope, resigned it to some special place for safekeeping, but the guard had no idea where. So every night after that, she would ask, until weeks had passed and the guard, a reliable fellow, finally ascertained where her harpsichord was.

The Prince of Fairmount's palace had four wings, one for each season. The Prince lived in the Eastern wing which had been decorated for the winter, with great white tapestries resembling snow drifts, and vases full of willow branches to represent the bare trees in the wintertime. Parthenope lived in the Western Wing, which was decorated for summer, with yellow and green tapestries and vases full of flowers of all kinds. The guard had learned from the majordomo that the harpsichord was in the Northern Wing, behind a great grille of iron and steel covered in roses, for in that wing was the great royal rose garden, itself a symbol of the spring.

Parthenope commanded the majordomo to show her the royal rose garden, but the majordomo refused.

'The royal rose garden,' the majordomo explained, 'is the sole property of the King and his heirs and is off-limits to the Queen and her retinue.'

'It is imperative that I must have my harpsichord,' Parthenope replied.

'I strongly suggest then, ma'am, that you take up this with His Royal Highness.'

When she did tell the Prince, he refused point-blank.

'What use do you have for such a worthless instrument? Such an instrument is only used to entice people into sin and error.'

Parthenope knelt down before the Prince, bowed her head and said most reverently: 'It is because that harpsichord is enchanted, and if I play it for you or anyone else, I can charm the winds and the waves to deliver up the treasures of the sky and sea.'

'How can this be?'

'Allow me to show you,' she replied.

So the Prince escorted her to the rose garden and opened up the great iron grille with a large set of keys. He took her gently by the arm and ambling around the great courtyard filled with roses of every kind and color, he took her to a chamber in the center of this vast rose garden. In this chamber were the relics of the martyrs, saints and heroes of the kingdom of Fairmount, and in the center of this holy chapel, Parthenope's beloved harpsichord. At once Parthenope sat at the keyboard and played a beautiful fantasia on a tune heard in the streets of Fairmount. The Prince was overcome with emotion. When she was done she looked up at him, but he had been so enthralled by the music, he was still in such a distracted state that he did not recognize her calling to him.

'My lord,' she said, 'get up and throw back the window, and look out upon the roses.'

When he did, he was astonished that they had all turned to gold.

'How did you accomplish such a feat?' The Prince said.

'This harpsichord is enchanted. It will give me everything you desire. Therefore, you must let me play it as much as I want.'

The Prince gladly accepted this proposition, and had the miraculous harpsichord moved to the Court of Honor. Whenever the Prince had a reception, he would bid Parthenope play. There all the people would see the miraculous things wrought by this harpsichord—gems and gold would pour from the fountains, fruit trees would mature and bear the most delicious fruit, the birds would accompany her in song, and everyone, from the most miserable beggar on the street to the Prince and all his royal household, at once had every comfort in the world.

Very soon the Prince's father the King, who was a very old man, died and the Prince was acclaimed as the new King of Fairmount. All the royal advisors met in the Hall of the Four Seasons in the center of the royal palace to discuss plans for the future. They were all in agreement that the King needed a royal heir, and it was time for Parthenope to accede to her role as Queen and give the King a son.

But Parthenope was still a virgin and had never been touched by a man. For in the kingdom of Fairmount there was a custom that man and wife not sleep together until a year and a day had passed between them in holiest chastity. On the night that the King desired Queen Parthenope to come to his bed, she prayed to God to help her. Inspired, she sat at her harpsichord and began to play it. The music rang through the entire palace and at once all the royal household fell into a deep sleep, and she was therefore able to avoid having to meet the King.

The next day he was very angry and commanded she be brought into his presence.

'You cannot refuse me,' the King said, furious. 'I have conquered lands and heathen foes, and I will not stand for palace intrigues to keep me from my duty in sustaining the kingdom.'

'But my lord,' she said, meekly, having prostrated herself on

the ground, 'you know how much I love my harpsichord. I can
do nothing else but play it. I promised you I could provide for
you as much as your heart desired. But I cannot provide you
with a son.'

'What madness is this that consumes you so? You spurn your
own husband and King for a madman's instrument? I have had
enough of this. Guards, clap her in the dungeon.'

The King of Fairmount also decreed that no one was to touch
the magical harpsichord, and to have it straightaway burned
in the public square. Parthenope was taken immediately to the
royal prison, where she was shut up in an oubliette filled with
unspeakably filthy and horrifying things.

For three days Queen Parthenope stayed there, until on the
third day, the King had her fished out. The guards threw a blue
robe over her and took her back to the royal palace, where she
was brought in fetters before the King.

'Now have you changed your mind, my lady? Will you aban-
don your awful frenzy, and accede to the role that Almighty
God has given to you?'

The guards pulled off the blue robe, and to their horror and
the astonishment of all the royal court they discovered that Par-
thenope had, in the course of three days, begun to change! Her
skin was beginning to turn pale and scaly, and she stank of fish.
Her face looked horribly marred. Her father's curse was begin-
ning to come true.

Astonished, the King sent for the Royal Doctor, but even
the most learned doctors could not explain her sickness. The
astrologer to the Court pronounced that the stars had aligned
in some unfortunate way and had afflicted the Queen with a
malady purely out of circumstance. Parthenope, however, knew
better.

The King repented of his cruelty and was full of remorse.

'My dear lady, my heart pains for you. I was foolish to think
that your father's curse were the ramblings of an insane fool.
I see the error of my ways! Tell me what you wish to have to

make you better, and I will give it to you.'

'Give me my harpsichord, and I will leave your presence and return to my father. I am of no use to you, for you cannot see the good that is within me. My beauty will fade, and I will die a mortal death, but the enchantment that is within me which sustains the realm can never die. Allow me to go in peace.'

Many people were dismayed when the Queen said this, because not only had Parthenope made it legal for women to play musical instruments in public, but now she was saying that she was more important than the King in playing her harpsichord. The Bishop and the royal advisors, then, planned to depose the Queen and finally destroy her instrument once and for all.

The King released the Queen from his custody and she returned to her quarters and found her harpsichord gone. The Bishop and the royal advisors had secretly removed it during the night. Another day passed and soon Queen Parthenope began to feel ill. She could not walk properly, and she found that she could not breathe anymore at night. Her ladies-in-waiting kept buckets to keep her wet during the night. And good Lord, she stank to high heaven! As the days passed, she grew weaker and more worried that her time might be coming to an end.

The next day after all this had transpired, the Holy Office came with a writ from the Archbishop, asking that she be put on trial for witchcraft.

The Bishop of Fairmount was invited to examine her, to see if she had been possessed by the Devil. The Bishop and his Inquisitors and the entire faculty of the University of Fairmount found that she presented no error in her thoughts or reasoning, nor any sort of heterodox belief contrary to those of the Church. But yet she was treated as a common malefactor of the worst sort.

The Holy Tribunal of the Inquisition on Fairmount held an auto-da-fé in front of the town hall and commanded the King to attend. On trial were two apostates and, believe it or not, the Queen herself. The Queen, very ill by this time, could barely utter a word of protest. One of the tribunal officials read the charge, and before the entire town, someone tossed a torch into the straw that surrounded her and the harpsichord.

At once Parthenope crawled through the flames to get to the harpsichord. Tongues of fire licked all around her, but it dared not to touch her enchanted body. She stood in the middle of the fire, and all her might, played out a fugue so elegant and beautiful that the fire danced in rhythm and turned on the guards. The flames arced over Parthenope and her beloved harpsichord, till at last, she emerged from the fire and the smoke, better than before! As the flames subsided she turned toward the astonished King, and said, 'You see what this harpsichord is capable of. Therefore, I beg you to let me keep it. You know I cannot give you a son. But I can give you the music that animates the world. I beg you, my lord, let me be free.'

The royal authorities were most certain that she was some sort of wicked enchantress and persuaded the Bishop that the marriage be annulled. The King acceded to their advice, as he could not jeopardize his claim on the crown. Instead, Queen Parthenope gave the King the most beautiful woman in all of Fairmount, the daughter of the Duke of Fruitland. They were married in a year, and she gave him thirteen beautiful sons and daughters, each of them the spitting image of their royal father. Two of his sons became Kings of Fairmount, while one became Bishop of Fountainvale and another the abbot of the Monastery of Thistlegrove.

The Bishop persuaded Parthenope to depart Fairmount once and for all, and to take her harpsichord with her. On her final day there, the King gave her a ship without a captain and bade her to charm the winds to return her home at her own peril. As she began to play the harpsichord a fine wind came from the south and blew all through the night, until after two days, she arrived back at the kingdom of Highcliff, where her father lived in his castle by the sea. But alas! —when she arrived at her father's tower, she found it but a pile of ruins. For when the man had given her away, he had willed himself over to death, and it was in his library, collapsed over a book of ancient spells, that she found he had breathed his last. She gave him a proper burial in the cave where her mother lay and then took all of the sacred books he owned and put it in her ship.

From there, she traveled west toward the blessed island of

Flowerfield, where she persuaded the abbess of the wealthy convent of Roseland to let her take vows. It was said that she stayed there the rest of her life, atoning for the sins of her father, but others said she played her harpsichord daily at Mass, thus enriching the abbey until it was so fabulously wealthy that even the roof of the church was made of pure gold.

When poor Parthenope was buried, the nuns found her legs covered in scales made of mother-of-pearl, hard as nacre and impossible to remove. Parthenope's harpsichord remained in the abbey church for many years, until one day, like many of the people and things in this story, it simply vanished into thin air and no one has been able to find it since.

The moral of the story, my dear children, is to never let anyone snuff out that most harmonious music that Almighty God has given to you, for it may very well astonish the whole world.

Droggoth

by Jonathan van Belle

"Droggoth, droggoth, feer'in spew, hrottest feeri'n spew thote burn allyn sins awayn.

Droggoth, droggoth, kommen hir to burn awoth allyn mine payn."

These lines from Altholm's *Morica* attest to the existence of the droggoth, whose habitation, though unknown today, is likeliest deep beneath the boreal forests of Medgidia in south-eastern Tromani. The 20th-century Tromani poet Dathomir is the last (presumed) eyewitness of the Droggoth. In his 1945 poem "Hateful Witness," Dathomir writes from the perspective of a "Droggothak," a person sentenced to that protracted and awful death by Droggoth (this particular Droggothak sentenced in the Medgidian "Trials" of January 1945):

> Burn away, once ripe, once effusive, once high spirit,
> For the clock's a cross, a crown of shed skin, its wages debts,
> Where the joy-bled end comes long before the worms.
>
> "Go away," the world would say, if it could speak,
> But the world is silent with idiot silence,
> Which some call love.
>
> Swaddle me in fire, that my body may bear true witness
> To the searing and sky-blackening it stored inside;
> But to whom my hateful witness?
>
> Gather my foul parts up for a pyre,
> For those children who love life still;
> Let them see me char that their little souls chill.
>
> Watch their child faces watch my body burn and you shall see:
> All hope in God is only disbelief
> That this world could be the atrocity that it seems.

The atrocity language is appropriate; the history of the Drog-
goth and its use in human affairs is described similarly by histo-
rian Anne Coleman as "indigestible atrocity." Altholm's *Morica*
is therefore ironic; the burning away of sin and pain being the
opposite of Droggoth's "hrottest feer'in" or hottest fire, which
rather magnifies pain. The anonymous 13th-century poem "De
Contemptu Mundi" ("On Contempt for the World") vividly
portrays this pain:

Thy fires flesh repair forever to feed thy fires forever;

The newborn touched writhes today an old man burning yet.

Contemptu ends, like Dathomir's "Hateful Witness," with a
theological question mark:

"Not God and Droggoth both," saith our wise;
"Deny the heart or doubt the eyes."

The Boy and the Tick

by Mickey Collins

One day a boy was sitting on a park bench, eyeing a girl across the way whom he loved. As he heaved another deep sigh over his lovelorn position, he heard a tiny voice ask him, "What's wrong, chum?"

The boy looked down to see a tiny tick on the bench next to him. He wasn't that surprised to hear a tick talking, it was the kind of world he lived in. "I sit here every day, across from that girl, and she has never noticed me."

"That's rough," said the tick. "As a tick, I can't really empathize. I do want to help you out though."

"You do? Why?"

"Well, I was going to suck your blood you see--I am a tick-- but it doesn't taste very good coming from a depressed person. How's about I help cheer you up and get her to notice you?"

"If you can get her to notice me, my heart would beat so fast I would have more than enough blood to share," said the boy. "You could have as much as you'd like. I'm Tom, by the way."

"Tock," said the tick. "Now, I'll just need a little bit of blood from you to get started."

Tom held out his pinky to Tock, who appreciatively sucked. "Come back tomorrow."

The next day when Tom sat on the bench he found a heart shaped out of sticks and mud the size of his palm.

"What do you think?" asked Tock the tick.

"It's very nice," said Tom, not wanting to offend. "But how will this get her to notice me?"

"Just go over there and give it to her. Girls love romantic gestures like that."

Tom looked over at the girl across the park, but his nerves got the best of him. "I can't go over there. Can't you build something that will make her come over here?"

Tock thought for a bit. "I suppose I could, but I would need some more help, and some more blood for my tick buddies."

Tom held out his fingers, and Tock and his tick friends each sucked on a finger, like kittens to their mother's nipples.

"See you tomorrow," said Tom, wiping his hand on his pants.

The next day Tom came to the park he found Tock and the ticks standing around sticks on the ground that formed "I <3 U." As Tom stood above it admiring the ticks' handiwork, he thought he saw the girl across the way look over and blush. But she still didn't leave her side of the park.

"Can you do bigger?" Tom asked.

"I've got more friends," said Tock. Tom was already holding out his hand. Tock and his friends swarmed up Tom's arm.

As Tom left the park, he felt slightly light-headed.

The next day Tom was feeling tired, but when he got to the park he felt much better. In front of his bench were ¾ replicas of him and the girl across the way. Tom was blown away with their work. And so was the girl, as she came over to him.

Tom's heart beat faster. He couldn't believe it. "Hello," she said.

Tom was speechless.

"Have you seen my dog?" she asked. He ran over here to play in that tall grass, but he's not coming when I call."

Tom said he hadn't seen her dog, but could help her look. As Tom made his way through the grass calling for the dog, he came across it. The dog was covered in ticks. "What the hell?" Tom whispered. "Tock, what's going on?" He started angrily brushing away the ticks covering the dog.

"We got so hungry building those statues of you and her that we needed more food."

"Not OK, Tock! She's really worried about her dog. Is it still alive?"

Tom picked up the dog.

"So you talked to her?" asked Tock. "That means the plan worked, and I fulfilled my end of the deal."

"Not now, Tock," said Tom. "I need to get this dog to the vet. We'll talk later."

Tom returned to the girl who was overjoyed to see her dog.

Tom and the girl did not return to the park the next day, nor the day after that. A week after the dog incident, Tock saw Tom and the girl walking together in the park with the dog. Tock scuttled up to Tom, who moved away from the girl to talk to Tock.

"We had a deal," said Tock. "I got her over to your side of the park, so you owe me as much blood as I would like."

"Can't it wait?" asked Tom. "I'm so busy and happy now."

Tock squinted his bug eyes at Tom in anger.

"Fine," said Tom and held out a finger.

Tock bit down and Tom flinched. The girl started calling for Tom.

"I'll be right there," said Tom. "Are you almost done?" he asked Tock.

Tock shook his head. The girl called again. Tom was getting impatient. He stood up and shook Tock off of his finger. "That seemed like a lot," said Tom. "We're even now."

But as Tock sat in the dirt, still hungry, he knew they were not even.

Several months later, Tom wheeled through the park to his bench. The statues and sticks were long scattered into shapeless piles. As he sat in his wheelchair, he looked across the park solemnly where the girl used to be with her dog.

"Hello chum," came a familiar tiny voice.

"Hey Tock," said Tom.

"Where's your girl?" asked Tock.

"She left me a while back. She saw all of the tick bites and thought they were hickies from other girls. And then I got Lyme disease." He motioned to his wheelchair.

"Tough break," said Tock.

"Can you do me one more favor?"

Tock was still resenting the interrupted lunch from long back, so he remained silent.

"I would like you to build a statue of her. One that's even stronger and bigger than before. Take as much blood as you'd like. It's the last thing I'd like to see before I die."

"A project that big will require a lot of blood," said Tock the tick. "Are you sure?"

Tom nodded.

Tock proceeded to bleed Tom dry, all on his own. But Tock was a tick of his word, and did build a statue of the girl. It was bigger and better than his previous works, but he was just a tick and didn't know much about building, so it fell apart within a day. It didn't matter, Tom was dead.

The moral of this story? Don't deal with blood-sucking insects.

Fairy Tale Dream
by Ula Jankowska

In my dream I am standing in a lake, water is dark and shallow, maybe a little thick. I am standing patiently waiting for things to happen when the first ghost shows up. He's wearing a colorful paper mask that is referring to Chinese mask traditions but the rest of his body is painted in geometrical patterns with white paint. His head looks like it's from Chinese theatre and his body looks like Paul Klee's work inspired by lost tribes body painting. He looks like nothing else I've ever seen but I'm waiting for him to come to me without any emotions. No fear, no excitement, deep internal calm. He is giving me a cup of coffee. Espresso is absolutely delicious, it's sweet, sour, bitter and salty, it has an interesting and round taste. Surprisingly even for me, I don't get excited about it. I feel thankful for this experience, nothing more than that. The second ghost has a different mask and is wearing clothes similar to those that the pope wears, but they are dark with traditional patterns, very similar to Aboriginal patterns. He gives me an old ashtray, which looks like it was just caught from the bottom of the sea. It's covered with mud. He gives it to me and I eat it. It's mostly unpleasant, as the ashtray smells exactly as ashtrays do, but it's crunchy, what surprises me a lot. I find this experience interesting as well.

When I wake up I decide to give up smoking.

Apple of My Eye
by Maya McOmie

I.

The forest darkens and

I know you wander it.

I hear bits of song, but

without recognizable

words—like the contents

of my own head.

Even in morning,

no warbles of birds,

only strange rustles

(leaves on branches?

Although they hang

blankly in winter.)

I hardly know you.

I can't remember

if I sit by a hearth,

or walk forever

among silent trees.

Imagine there must

be some reason

for lingering here,

waiting for something.

I know it is not

you I wait for—

yet sonic memory, as if

your shadow, a recurring

theme, catalyst to

dreams.

     Whatever agony,

terror defracts in eyes'

nooks—filed away

quickly—doesn't hit

anymore; although perhaps

I should not

so easily refurbish:

anger, alarm, rapture.

II.

You might call me foolish,

temperamental—but

that isn't the story

I am telling.

You barely register

as steadfast; neither

do easy lies draw me

into the cavernous well.

It is only in stories

I believe gap-riddled

capes like that. I grasp this,

in my head. But there

(I deceive myself)

you gave me such

a look; I'm not sure

any more what

part is myth, what

part spirals.

                    Are

these always so

entwined together,

ensnared? It's not

just the wall of bramble,

impossible to hack through,

which intrigues me.

Hear this missive:

I won't be the damsel

you use to escape

your unhappy beginning.

I'm not the catalyst

to your plot. And I don't

need 50 mattresses.

I have the apple and

I don't care much for it.

III.

The apple tastes

mealy; ashen

and hard to identify,

with barely a taste.

As if the tongue

steps blindfolded.

Not that I expect

pleasantness these days.

I can't say I know

what to expect.

Unlike what people

have said about me,

I know I shouldn't eat

it. I know what they

say about girls

like me. All ebony

and snow. I am not

about to blame it

on my looks. Yes;

I do know; it is why

I am doing it.

Still, I do not

crave banishment.

I do not know what

happens after

leaving the garden.

Or what is left

at chilly doorsteps;

the unopened, unordered

parcel. I no longer

wish to unsee what

the serpent

has told me.

I no longer dread

what emerges

when dusk has passed,

entering the light

after all the whole sky

has hit its peak.

I'm tired, can't that

be enough?

I don't want a world

where everything

exists within reason.

The Fox

by Azalea Micketti

The house was tall and white, a handsome porch stretching the length of the front in support of a balcony above. It was an old house, but it had aged well, supported by the inhabitants and the healthy soil beneath. That same soil supported a multitude of fruit trees, spread out before the house like so much jam. There were pears and apples and cherries, and even a few apricots and plums.

There was a Fox that lived in this orchard. He hadn't been invited, but when does that ever stop a fox. He was lead to the house by the sound of chickens. And chickens there were, but they were well protected, better than most. The Fox liked a challenge and had come back several days in a row in an attempt to catch one off guard. Unfortunately for him, the woman who lived in the house was not easily distracted, and the Tomten who usually hid himself in the shed had taken to sleeping inside the coop, in order to protect his charges.

The Fox was frustrated. Never once had he thought about making his way towards the front of the house, until one day he had heard dogs barking and caught the scent of a new human. Curious, he snuck around the side of the house and yipped in shock. There were two enormous wolfhounds on the front walk. The Fox almost bolted, but for the woman who stood on the steps before them. Her long dark hair trailed down her back, and she went barefoot. More interesting than either of these things, she held a dead bird in one hand.

She called out to the man holding the two dogs. He shouted back before pulling his snarling canines down the path and through the gate. The Fox kept his eyes on the dogs as they left, then glanced up to see what the woman would do. She was standing on the porch, directly above him. This time he did yip, and leapt back.

"So you're the one who's been threatening my chickens," she said. She did not seem angry, but the Fox could never be sure. He breathed deeply and for the first time caught a nose full of the woman's scent. She smelled of earth and herbs and time. There was something comforting and familiar about her, though the Fox knew she was a stranger to him.

"I'll make you a deal," she said. "Stay away from my chickens, and I'll make sure you never go hungry." She paused for a moment and the Fox continued to watch her. "What do you think, Tom?" She looked up and before he could stop himself the Fox glanced over his shoulder as well. The Tomten was standing at the corner of the house behind him.

"Sounds fair to me," he said. His voice sounded like snow falling on aspens and water trembling over a riverbed; as though all his years had been set down in a single book and the pages carefully riffled by a stiff breeze.

The Fox glanced back up at the woman. She was holding out the bird for him to take. The Fox glanced between the two of them again, nostrils testing the air around him. Without warning, he darted forward, stole the bird and ran.

"How long?" she asked Tom.

"I wouldn't be surprised if he comes poking around again tonight. Voracious things, foxes." The woman chuckled, then she turned around and went back inside.

*

The house was old, but the woman was older. She had been old when the house was built. By human standards she was impossibly old, though she appeared to be in her mid-30s. While she told most people the house had been built by her grandmother, the truth was she had built it herself, her grandmother being who-knew-where at that point. Probably sleeping with the King of England.

While she had lived there for many years, she had not always "lived" there. She lived there as herself now, or as much of herself as she felt like sharing. But at one point she had been he, or them, or a different version of her. It did no one good to have the same woman living alone in that house for over 200 years. Besides, had she lived as openly as she did now, even 50 years ago, she probably would have been run out of town. Or at least she would have found herself replacing the windows more often than she'd like.

Now, however, seemed like as good a time as any to truly enjoy the fruits of many lifetimes–both literal and metaphorical–and the particularly sensual nature of this one. The man who had just left had once been a lover of hers. So had the man who fetched her mail. And the woman at the library. And that lovely young couple who used to live next door. But if she stopped to contemplate the entire list of previous bedfellows, she could be here all day.

She took care of the house in the same way that the house took care of her. She kept it clean and well-groomed, and full of life. There were three cats who lived in the house, and who had lived on the land before there was a house to live in. She would not call them her cats, for she did not own them and they would never consent to being owned by anyone. But they lived harmoniously, she providing food, they providing pest control and certain magical qualities.

Apart from the chickens and the cats there were a number of other creatures who visited frequently. A pair of ravens, a murder of crows, occasional doves and pigeons. There was a family of hedgehogs living at the bottom of the garden, and earlier in the year there had been a skunk and her babies. Life thrived around the little house. Insects and arachnids and worms crawled all over the plants. Sugar ants crept through the cracks in the windows, and butterflies danced around the rose bushes. The motley collection of living things filled to bursting the house, the garden, the orchard, but there was a sense of balance about it all, as though each individual had it's place and worked to create a cohesive whole.

The neighbours did not always understand this carefully struck balance, and more than once had, unknowingly, worked to throw it out of joint.

*

It was late. Past midnight, closing in on 1 am, and the house was asleep. The garden and the orchard were alive with noc-

turnal creatures eating and mating and creating life. But inside
the house was dark, and still, and quiet. The Fox crept around
the outside towards the front and that spectacular orchard. He
had been dreaming of those trees all day long. The Fox was not
new to dreams, but this dream had been so real he could smell
the scent of ripe fruit and feel the breeze in his fur. He wanted
nothing more than to return, possibly forever.

As he came level with the front porch the Fox paused, lis-
tening. There was something out there in the darkness. That
something was crying. There was something in the sound that
twisted at the Fox's heart, making him sink farther into the
long grass. After a moment the Fox saw a figure slowly mak-
ing its way down the stone pathway. It got closer and the Fox
saw that it was a woman, her face stained with tears, white hair
shining in the light of the crescent moon. He watched closely
as she stumbled up the stairs, ears pricked for any other sounds
in the night. As the woman crossed the porch the Fox glanced
past her and saw another set of eyes and a soft red cap peeking
over the opposite edge of the porch. Their eyes met and the Fox
lifted his brows. The Tomten raised his own in return.

As they watched, the woman on the porch raised a hand to
knock at the door, and hesitated. Another sob rocked her body
and as she gasped for breath the wind began to blow.

The Fox heard a sound from inside the house. Footsteps. They
hurriedly descended the stairs and raced towards the door. In
a moment it was flung wide and the woman who lived in the
house threw her arms around the woman on the porch.

The woman who lived in the house had also been dreaming.

The woman on the porch sobbed into her shoulder, the
sound of her grief echoed by the wind and carried through the
orchard till every tree trembled. The woman who lived in the
house stroked the other woman's white hair and rubbed her
shoulders, murmured soft comforting words, and slowly pulled
her across the threshold. The door was shut, and once more the
night fell quiet.

The Fox and the Tomten shared a look. The breeze had died
as the women entered the house, and the darkness was incred-

ibly still, as though the entire world was holding its breath. And
then, as though some 'all clear' had been sounded, the orchard
came to life again. The Tomten turned his back and returned
to the chickens. The Fox proceeded into the orchard. Almost at
once, he began to dig.

*

The house was used to tears.

Tears, sweat, blood, shit. These were the things that humans
were made of, and the house was more than familiar with hu-
mans.

The woman who lived in the house lead the other woman
upstairs to a spare room. She took off her shoes, she braided
her hair, and tucked her into the wide bed, all the while singing
softly under her breath.

The other woman gasped, choking on tears. She tried to
speak.

"She's gone," she whispered. The woman who lived in the
house tried to shush her, but she spoke again. "They're all gone."
The other woman reached a hand out to the woman who lived
in the house, and as her fingers brushed the woman's cheek they
both began to weep.

*

When the Fox awoke in the early evening, he was immedi-
ately aware of voices. He was well concealed in the den he had
dug the night before, cradled between the roots of an enormous
apple tree. He pricked his ears and listened. The woman and an-
other human. Perhaps the friend from the night before? Curios-
ity overtook him and he crawled out of his hole.

The breeze from the previous night had stuck around, and the
branches of the fruit trees waved sporadically as the Fox slunk
towards the house. 50 paces from the porch he sank to his belly
in the grass and watched the two women as they talked. After a
moment he became aware of a most delicious smell, and lifted
his nose into the wind. Something with meat and spices and

root vegetables. It smelled warm and delicious and full of fat. Abandoning instinctual precautions, he slithered on his belly towards the house and that wonderful smell.

As the Fox got closer the woman who lived in the house pulled a dish off the table beside her and descended the three steps into the grass. The fox froze. She took a careful step to the side, set the dish on the ground, and turned away. When she was once more tucked into her chair, deep in conversation, the Fox took a breath. His nostrils were once more flooded with that heavenly scent. He crept forward again.

As the Fox ate he watched closely, ears twitching forward and back, picking up every little sound carried by the wind. The woman with the white hair was no longer crying, but she smelled salty and sad. She smiled now and again, but the Fox did not know if this was good or bad. He ate his food in silence, hearing birds call overhead and the rumble of cars on the road behind him.

Suddenly the woman who lived in the house sat up straight, dark hair lifting away from her face in defiance of gravity. There was a new sound from behind the Fox and he looked around, dish empty and nearly forgotten. A man was standing outside the gate to the orchard. He was tall and broad and wore a wool flat cap pulled low over his face. The Fox could smell something metallic and putrid, and there was a darkness that hung about him like a shroud.

"You are not welcome here," the woman said. She did not raise her voice, she did not stand, she simply spoke as though the man was beside her. The man lifted his head and when the Fox saw his eyes he hissed. The woman stood, and the Fox heard the Tomten approaching from the back of the house.

The air crackled with electricity. The cool breeze was suddenly hot and dry, the leaves in the trees grating against one another furiously. Clouds began to gather above the house, flickers of lightening manifesting in their depths.

"You are not welcome here." This time the woman's voice was powerful and was accompanied by a resounding clap, as though a massive door had been shut above their heads.

The man tipped his hat, and shuffled his boots on the side-walk, and disappeared.

The electricity slowly dissipated, the breeze returning to its former temperature. The clouds, however, continued to build and glower down upon them until the horizon was filled with steel grey monstrosities of condensed moisture.

The woman's hair was now held aloft only by the natural physics of curly hair in high humidity. Her dark curls bounced around her face as she looked up at the sky.

"I think it is time to go in," she said. She ran down into the grass to grab the empty dish as the woman with the white hair picked up the two mugs on the table and went inside. The Fox fled as soon as she approached, and was gone before they entered the house. The moment the woman's heel left the porch it began to rain.

*

It was still raining at midnight, and the Fox was regretting not having dug his den a little deeper under the roots of his chosen apple tree. The orchard soaked up the water like a man dying of thirst. The tree provided some cover, though the drops were thick and they quickly saturated the ground. The smell of damp earth mixed with damp canine was pungent and nearly over-whelming.

Although the rain was loud, the Fox's ears were sharp and he heard the Tomten coming across the lawn well before he arrived. Of course, the Fox now realized that the only reason he could hear him at all was because the Tomten wanted to be heard. He slowly made his way across the wet grass, and as the Fox peeked out of his den he could see the way the Tomten's red hat strained under the weight of so much water, and his eyebrows sparkled with droplets. The Fox could smell fresh hay mixed with the Tomten's own scent of woodsmoke and age. He stopped under the adjacent plum tree and beckoned.

The Fox did not move.

The Tomten beckoned again more urgently. When the Fox

did not respond he called, "There is plenty of room in the shed where it is warm and dry. Come." When the Fox still didn't move he turned his back and walked away. The Fox watched as he made his slow progress back across the wet orchard, water dripping from the tip of his weeping hat. The Tomten reached the edge of the house and just before he disappeared the Fox darted out and dashed across the grass. His belly was soon damp with rain and his ears dripped. Rounding the edge of the porch he saw the Tomten disappearing around the opposite corner into the back yard. He followed quickly, squeezing himself as close to the house as possible to avoid more raindrops.

He paused again at the end of the house and hesitantly peered into the yard. The shed sat against the back fence, next to the chicken coop, which was locked up tight against the rain. The door to the shed was ajar, and a warm light spilled out into the thunderous night. Exhaling a cloud of steam the Fox ran towards the door, picking up the scent of hay again, this time mixed with the earthy smell of damp soil and chickens.

He peeked around the door.

Inside the Tomten was laying out a blanket on top of a pile of soft hay. There were more blankets folded neatly beside him, and an oil lamp hanging from a hook on the wall. The Fox crept silently inside and stood dripping in the doorway. The Tomten turned and, picking up a second blanket, made his way over. He encouraged the Fox farther into the shed, and once in, shut out the rain. The Tomten held up the blanket. The Fox looked at it blankly.

"Stand in the corner and shake. Then I will dry your ears." The Fox slunk into the far corner of the shed as the Tomten held the blanket up to protect himself from the spray of water. As the Fox shook, creating a mini imitation of the storm outside, the lamp flickered and thunder rolled. Creeping back towards the door, the Fox stood tensely as the Tomten gently dried his ears, then his tail, then lay the blanket on the floor for him to wipe his paws.

Satisfied, the Fox trotted over to the nest the Tomten had created and made himself comfortable. Curling himself into a ball, he pricked his ears toward the Tomten in a silent question.

"The chickens are safe enough without me tonight. I think I will sleep in my own bed." The Fox watched closely as the Tomten lay the wet blanket over a bale of hay to dry, then, taking a third blanket from the pile, took it over to a much more well established nest in the corner. The Tomten blew out the lantern as he went, and they both lay in the dark for a moment, listening to the rain.

"Sleep," the Tomten said. And the Fox did just that.

*

The rain was paler in the morning light, and a great deal of the moisture had taken to the air in the form of mist. Despite his keen eye sight, the Fox could barely see across the yard towards the kitchen. The door was open, and there was light and sound and the most heavenly aroma erupting from it. The fox could hear the woman and the Tomten speaking to each other, but could not understand their words.

There was a cluck-cluck beside him and he glance over to see the chickens sleepily emerging from their coop. Instinct kicked in and the Fox crouched low against the dirt, ears up, tail back. He scented the air and took a careful step forward.

"Don't even think about it." The Fox's ears went back in surprise. He looked around the yard. There was no one there. He paused for a moment before his gaze went back to those vulnerable birds and he crept a couple steps closer.

"I can see you." This time the Fox lay flat on his belly, ears flat against his head, letting out a little huff of air that stirred the cold ground before him. He glanced back over at the kitchen and saw the woman peering out at him through the kitchen door. She winked and turned her back. Suddenly the Fox remembered her promise. He hesitated for a moment before hopping up and trotting toward the open door.

Poking his nose around the door frame, he saw the Tomten sitting on a small stool beside a large iron stove. He was carefully packing tobacco into a long pipe made out of some kind of horn while the women chopped something on the high table that ran the length of the room. The Fox was too short to see what they were doing, but he could smell something savoury and sharp. The Fox made to step farther into the room and froze.

There was a cat sitting underneath the table.

They stared at each other for a moment, neither daring to move, neither willing to back down. The cat kneaded its paws against the flagstones and lowered itself. The Fox did not move.

"Pearl," the woman said, not looking up from her work. "The Fox is our guest." If cats could roll their eyes, Pearl certainly would have. Instead she adopted the half-lidded gaze of utter indifference and after a moment appeared to doze off entirely.

The Fox set his foot down. He glanced up at the woman, who was not looking at him, then at the Tomten, who was now lighting his pipe. With an imperceptible shrug the Fox made his way over to the stove and plopped down beside it, making sure he still had a clear view of the cat under the table.

They stayed like that for a long time. The Tomten smoking his pipe, the cat dozing under the table, the Fox gently steaming beside the stove. The two women moved around them, chopping simmering, boiling, roasting, baking. They seemed to be making enough food for an army, or the entire winter. After a while the woman set a plate of meat scraps on the floor in front of the Fox, who immediately sat up and devoured the offering.

The cat got her own small plate but, unlike the fox, did not touch it. At least, not until the Fox started to creep towards it himself. Then she gave him a glare and ate everything on the plate as slowly as she could. The Fox went back to his spot by the stove and watched closely.

The kitchen was so warm, and the Fox was so full, that after a while—and against his better judgement—he began to doze. He dreamed of geese and ravens and the sweet slide of egg down his throat. He was running. Running through a forest. He could hear dogs behind him, baying for his blood.

*

In the kitchen the Tomten watched as the Fox twitched in his sleep, letting out a small whimper.

"Dreaming?" the woman asked. The Tomten nodded, still watching.

"He is being hunted." The Tomten finally said. The woman froze, a knife still in her hand. "In the dream it is by dogs. In reality…" he trailed off. The two women exchanged a look, hands paused above their work, watching the Fox through the haze of steam that permeated the kitchen.

"The mugwort is about to boil." In a flash, everyone was in motion again. The woman continued chopping, her friend stirred one of the large pots, and the Tomten re-lit his pipe. He exhaled a large cloud of smoke, watching the Fox with interest.

*

The Fox awoke with a start. The kitchen was dark except for the wood stove, and the Fox could smell something softly bubbling in a pot on top. Pricking his ears he could hear the sound of voices coming from the front room of the house. Many voices. Springing to his feet the Fox tiptoed through the interior door and into a darkened hallway. With silent steps he made his way deeper into the house.

*

The Tomten peered around a bedroom door as the Fox passed, but the Fox did not see him. Tom watched as the fox was drawn farther down the hall, toward the chanting that drifted back from the living room. The Tomten followed the Fox, taking care not to make a sound.

*

The door at the end of the hallway was ajar, and the Fox carefully stuck his nose in the gap, prying it open. The door let out a soft sigh and opened just enough for the Fox to peer through into the front room.

There were nine women, sitting in a circle, hands joined,

softly chanting. A few drops of rain pattered against the windows at the front of the room, but the women remained sitting, eyes closed, breathing softly into the candlelight. The pattering grew in frequency and volume, and soon the rain was pounding against the windows like fists, demanding to come in. The Fox carefully pushed the door wider and sat in the frame, watching silently.

Suddenly, though nothing changed, something was different. The air began to hum, soon matching the rain volume for volume. The pounding of raindrops was now joined by the actual pounding of fists on the door. Every hair on the Fox's body stood on end and he leapt to his feet, eyes locked on the door.

And then the Tomten was behind him. The Fox jumped as the Tomten passed him and skirted the outside of the circle before standing in front of the heavy door. The pounding came louder and the Fox could see the door shaking in its frame. He stood, unsure what to do. Every instinct was telling him to run, to sprint down the hallway and out through the kitchen door and away. But he knew he would never escape. That pounding might as well be the baying of hounds. He knew what it meant. He knew it was for him.

The Fox stepped forward into the room, and the woman who lived in the house looked over at him from her place in the circle. He could see the candlelight reflecting in the depths of her eyes, and felt himself drawn to her. He padded toward the circle, feet shuffling against ancient floorboards. The humming was beginning to recede and the rain lessen, but still there was that pounding fist. The Fox paused at the very edge of the circle of clasped hands. He could smell the sweat of many bodies and something metallic and salty. Hesitantly he raised a foot to step into the circle.

There was a pause in the pounding.

In the silence the Fox could hear every single heart beat in the room. Nine women, one Tomten, one Fox. There was no heartbeat on the other side of the door. The pounding resonated through the room, vibrating through the floorboards, and the Fox startled. The woman had not taken her eyes off of him, and he met her gaze once more as he stepped into the circle.

There was a rush of wind down the chimney and the fire guttered, the candle flames dancing and flickering madly. The wind outside scrapped branches against the side of the house and threw more rain at the windows. There was a moaning that seemed to echo from the upper stories of the house; a whistling of unsealed windows that sounded like terrible cries.

The Fox made his way into the centre of the circle, directly across from the woman who lived in the house. He could feel the house itself stretching and breathing around him, trying to expel the poison from its veins. He had been so focused on the woman that he did not notice that there was something inside the circle until he nearly tripped over it. Glancing down he saw a small obsidian bowl, full to the brim with clear water. Standing directly over it, the Fox could see his reflection in its surface. The face the stared back at him was not his own.

The Fox jumped back with a start, looking back up at the woman. She was now inside the circle with him, the other eight woman having closed the gap behind her in order to maintain its integrity. She remained perfectly still, sitting at the edge, watching him. The Fox began to pace. He wanted to get out, he wanted to run, to flee. But there was something that wouldn't let him. Perhaps the continued pounding on the door, or perhaps something deeper within him, something he could not name.

A spark ran down his spine and he yipped in pain. Digging his claws into the floor he barked and shrieked as his skin crawled and twisted around him. The pounding from outside answered his cries with an increase in volume, and he clenched his teeth in an effort to keep quiet. He didn't want it to hear him, to find him. He glanced up again, a growl rumbling low in his chest. The woman was closer now, and she had placed something on the floor in front of her. Two things now sat between them: the bowl, and a large black candle. The flame danced as the Fox growled. The woman reached across the candle toward the Fox, something held carefully in her fist.

Before the Fox could blink she opened her fist and dropped a stone into the bowl of water.

The water exploded outward, drenching both Fox and woman, extinguishing the candle with a hiss. For a moment the Fox wondered how such a small bowl could hold so much liquid. But then the darkness overwhelmed him and he thought no more. The Fox collapsed. There was a sucking sound as air rushed back out through the chimney and the cracks in the walls.

The pounding stopped.

The wind stopped.

The chanting stopped.

The candles were still, the only sound that of raindrops and heartbeats.

The woman looked over at the Tomten who still stood in front of the door. He carefully placed a hand against the wood, listening with ears more sensitive then any wild creature's. After a moment of silence the Tomten turned back to the room and sighed. He nodded at the woman who breathed in with relief. Gesturing at two of the other women in the circle she said, "Carry him into the spare bedroom and lay him on the bed." The women stood immediately to obey, gathering him up between the two of them, one under the shoulders one under the knees. The Tomten lead the way up to the second floor of the house as the rest of the women began to set the room back on its feet.

*

When he awoke there was sun shining on his face. Blinking in the brightness of early morning sun, he glanced towards the open window. A fragrant breeze was pushing its way past the sheer curtains, trying to fill the room with the scent of cherry blossoms. His head was resting on a soft pillow, and as he turned to look around the room he realized he was covered by a quilted comforter. He tried to sit up, but the mechanics of it were wrong and he fell back against the pillow. His hips and shoulders were in the wrong place, flattened somehow. And sore.

He closed his eyes again and breathed in. Other than the smell of cherry blossom the only other thing he could identify was his own scent. But even that smelled different.

He opened his eyes again with a snap and glanced towards the door. The woman who lived in the house was standing on the threshold, studying him carefully.

"Good morning," she said in a quiet voice. "Do you remember last night?" He blinked at her a moment, frozen in fear, every muscle in his body tense. He shook his head. She nodded, but didn't seem surprised.

"You were cursed." At the word cursed, something of the night before came rushing back to him, though it was mostly dark impressions and terror. Instinct took over and he threw the covers off and jumped down, intending to bolt from the room. His muscles gave out and he promptly collapsed onto the floor. The woman chuckled.

"Two legs will take a little getting used to, so I'd take it easy if I were you." She reached down towards him and he scrambled away across the floor as best he could. The air was cool on his skin and his limbs felt clumsy and out of joint. The woman had paused when he pulled away, and for a moment stood as still as a statue.

"Are you hungry?" she asked. Not taking his eyes off her he nodded. She nodded in return and left the room, closing the door behind her.

He sat on the floor, completely naked, and studied his hands. He flexed his feet. He rubbed his butt against the soft carpet. He clenched his hands into fists, then extended his fingers as far as they would go. The breeze tickled the sparse hairs on his arm and he shivered. The door of the room opened again and the woman stood there with a bowl and a spoon.

He opened his mouth. He cleared his throat.

"What happened?" he asked.

Two-Headed Troll

by Robert Eversmann

A two-headed troll pushes through the trees and finds a heart. A heart as big as a boulder or horse. The heart there beating on the ground, bright red pinned in the grass in the moonlight. Akork and Bagork. One reaches but his other stays his hand.

--I want the heart and I deserve the heart.

--No, I will put it into my chest because my life is harder than yours.

Akork lifts the left arm. Bagork lifts the right. They stretch. They rock their shoulders back. If they take the heart, they will become two. Two heads. Two hearts. They regard it now like a widening hole or bleeding animal.

--We are too woefully the same. I hate you, Bagork.

Bagork cries. Agork lends his hand to wipe away tears. Same shadow. Same arms.

--I will take the heart and put it in my chest. It needs a body.

--But what if we are turned to stone?

--Put the heart in me. Do you remember the little farmer? I loved the little farmer.

--You ate him.

-- I deserve the heart. I deserved the little farmer. I will touch the heart. It will beat inside me.

A troll needs only a second heart. But where did this one come from? Another dead troll. The trolls, two of them making the operations as smoothly as one, though each looking his own direction, one at the sky, reflecting maybe on all their life to-gether, the other at the heart, paling, dying, beating there slowly like the split chest of a horse.

The troll slumps their one set of shoulders. Akork agog, Akork ready, Akork beating his heart, their heart, with his fist of tear-wet fingers, his chest, their chest, he beats it and beats it.

--The same heart in our body. One heart. Our heart. Two hearts.

--I will put it in you.

Akork stops. There will be no more Akork and Bagork. There will be no more two-headed troll, there can be no two-hearted troll. It is impossible. And now this too-giant heart. Bagork reaches, caresses it, says to Akork, It's ok, reach your hand out. And the trolls pick it up between them, their two gentle hands, this new heart shivering birdlike in their warmth. Two thumbs meet atop the puckering left ventricle. Akork and Bagork lock eyes.

--There's no going back.

--I know.

They push the heart into Akork's mouth. Blood runs down his chin, tilting to the moon, blood streaming, blood running down their chest, their legs, blood staining and piling in the grass. Akork chews the heart and Bagork watches him.

--Do you feel different?

--Yes.

An instant fracture like a bolt struck between them. Now growing. Two new arms, two new legs, two trolls birthed like stone, cracking, shattering, forming. What once was one now is two. Sunlight threatens through the forest. Two trolls flee, away from each other, away from the grass, flayed damp like a pile of men.

Happily Never After
by Jaya Blackburn

happily never after

shadow fairies

with pointed tails

yeah

like the devil

their t-shirts proclaim

'death saves'

as they dance

through dark hallways

yeah

in my mind

i catch

tiny glimpses

mesmerizing phrases pulled backwards

through ruby red lips

forked tongues

slither through my psyche

whispering

promises

of happily

never after

your turn

the dark forest invitations

have been sent

your presence has been requested

at the banquet

to dine

on poison apples

and voodoo

so sweet

cookies say 'eat me'

so you do

and you realize

the Dark Prince

sitting next to you

lips like red red roses

thorns tattooed

and his neck

bleeds your name

another stranger arrives

carrying red red roses

for your casket

you feebly dispute

their necessity

as the Dark Prince

looks at you

quietly smiling

have you eaten

he asks

we really should get going

all the arrangements have been made

and others are awaiting their turn

wandering nightly

circles serenade the moon

drumbeats in shadows

escapades slip

through the centers of stars

magic incantations

to open new worlds

peel back the myth

expose the lust

excursions and dimensions

for desirous playthings

creatures of habit

wandering nightly

into the forest

to lick at the edges

slip into your dreams

forever faithful

to fantasies

and nightmares

come true

The Weaver and the Swarm

by Timothy Merritt

They live in the eyes. At the edge of every field of vision they wait just beyond the periphery, ever eager and always hungry. They teeter on the edge of each glance, relishing the moment when a view shifts and they are free to perform their sole function. That which is passed over by the perpetually wandering eye is devoured to the last, an instant after being replaced with a new angle. They are the straggling swarm, lingering around every stare, waiting at the rims of awareness.

They are the gluttons of the unseen, purveyors of all distraction, the eaters of that which is previous. They hide so well, in part, because of the inherent deficit in perception. We see only that pinpoint of central focus where we train our sight, the single word in a sea of phrases, while our minds do their best to appease us in thinking we have more of the picture. An unreliable recall fills in the surrounding dimness, illuminating the rest of the page and the world around it from memory—mostly, from approximation. Surety is alluded to, where truly there is only the unknown. But this optic fallacy only serves to conceal, a safety blanket against that jibbering swarm of strangers to salience, who rend the remnants left behind after each glancing look.

And while these ocular accoutrements serve well enough as nourishment for the ravenous creatures of the orb, it is the less tangible ideas at the foundation of those banally pictured forms—fear, love, hatred, rapture—that better quell the ache of an infinite hunger, if only for a fleeting moment. Those primordial elements that construct the view seeking to reframe chaos as order, formless notions wrapped round the psyche as a thin membrane of defense against the constant truth of oblivion, these are the choicest bites that are consumed, whether our eyes see or not (for even the blind take in a contrived view of a universe built on rules, and all thinking beings are subject to those most primal of emotions; there is food for the swarm in all of us).

Yet they are faultless in their motives, only fulfilling the function of their design. Their insatiability is but one half of balanced symbiosis, a dance that creates as well as destroys. Their more obscured compatriot lives deep within the black void of the unconscious, down a long winding path of branching uncertainties beyond the amygdala, where it governs the synthesis of pure primal fear. Uninhibited by the higher, and thus more convoluted, functions of the mind, it draws best from the unadulterated terror of the unknown—cosmic insignificance and mortal impermanence—to build a lie of sight. It is the weaver of worldviews, spinning forth a story that can be comprehended, tangible in its rules and aesthetics (though these too are illusions) to mask amorphous fear with a temporarily logical structure. To the swarm, it is a weaver of sustenance, a hand that feeds.

Without the weaver all existence would stay a mad, roiling incongruity. Meaning would remain unborn, and any semblance of sense-making would be alien in its processes. The weaver spins for every conscious cog in the cosmic machine, allowing existential pain to be repressed, condensed, and woven into more palatable patterns. Without its work, there would be no coherency in the mind, no chance for rumination. That fragile frame it constructs, however false it might be, allows an added breath to be drawn, a moment of steadying to take place at the precipice of the void (wherein all the wonders of creation are born), and it is from these wonders the weaver takes inspiration when it threads those most unruly tapestries of all: the dreams of the sentient. Here it sprinkles glittering jewels, whose gleaming remains even after the swarm has torn them from their slumbered settings.

Yet the weaver too knows its place within the cycle. The swarm must be nourished. To buck that responsibility is to risk the addled uprising of each straggling eater, and those instances are always catastrophic. Without its steadying falsehoods woven before each probing look, the dependent mind and its owner are obliterated, sent free-falling back into that unfiltered nothingness that devours more greedily than any swarm.

Sometimes, though, there is cause to be frugal in its artistry. Occasionally the weaver will allow only the thinnest of tapestries to shield a mind's eye from the underlying calamity, and on these occasions the viewer is treated to a framework translucent enough to allow in flickers of cosmic truth—and as such, cosmic madness. These minds are obliterated more often than not, but a select few endure this wider view and sometimes even thrive under it, becoming conduits for ideas beyond the scope of more obfuscated intellects. Whether the weaver does this for sport, malice, or by some higher directive is not known, but there is seemingly no presentiment regarding which mind receives a thinner veil.

The cycle lasts a lifetime. One side synthesizes terror and chaos into false mosaics of causality, of an existence that our rudimentary minds can accept for an infinitesimal glimpse. The other destroys and digests the intricacy back into an ethereal energy, unraveling and transmuting the work of the weaver to its original shapeless malleability. They work in tandem, a dyad of unseen forces held together by the tension of the human condition, until the eyes close for a final time and the swarm is permitted to gorge itself ceaselessly on the last fading vestiges of consciousness, their duty done and their bellies full.

So be mindful of the weaver and the swarm. When you feel prickles at the edge of your vision, or an itching in the under-current of your consciousness, rest assured it is only the churning of the swarm laying waste to a moment you've left behind. And when you find yourself consumed with strange, terrifying thoughts, or plagued with the notion that something is funda-mentally wrong in your life, know that the weaver is gifting you a prized peek into infinity, well worth a moment's look, even if it destroys you in the end.

Lust Fish

by Ariel Kusby

A young maiden with a secret: inside her chest, beneath her lace blouse, her rouged skin, and ribcage like a lobster trap, a carp lay flapping. At night it thumped against her sternum, keeping her awake. It bullied her, beating air out of her lungs, warning her against many men who she encountered and thought of in the night. On the occasion she brought a lover to her bed, eventually their chests would press together, and he would feel it. Something clammy, a slapping fish. Lovers left her one by one, feeling uneasy, unable to say exactly what had turned them off, other than that it seemed like something cold lay beneath the maiden's breasts. At the carp's urging she'd soak in the bathtub, where she would cry and wonder how she'd ever kill it.

The carp thrived on water, so she tried to dehydrate herself. Still, red tides of blood would rescue the carp, which still would have swum in the dried-up puddle of her dead body, if it could. She consumed massive amounts of special algae and root vegetables known to be toxic to fish. Still, it flipped and squirmed, pushing the poison back up out of her body. She looked for fishermen everywhere she went, soliciting hooks. Even when she found them, the carp would not bite. One day, the carp murmured, *I am your mother.* Sure she had gone mad, the young maiden ran to the nearest lake, where she threw herself into the water. *You are lucky I did not lock you up in any tower other than your own body*, the carp screamed. The young maiden dove deep into the lake, pulling water into her lungs, forcing her body further and further down into the darkness.

Near the muddy tar of the lake bottom, her body went limp and her blood took on so much water that the fish broke from its cage and swam freely through her corpse. As it pushed up into the maiden's throat it propelled her body forward, skimming the lake scum. The carp grew and shapeshifted, occupying her body and moving it at its will. A ghoulish siren transformed, animated by the carp that now claimed the lake as its own domain, haunting the forests of muskgrass, disrupting algal blooms, and knocking frogs from their perches.

In spite of the schools of small fish it terrorized, within weeks, the carp quickly grew restless. The lake was too quiet. The maiden's body was a powerful, yet boring vessel. At any sign of movement the carp would jump, and tear a smaller fish to pieces. Early one morning a sudden plop on the surface: a shiny yellow creature, a snake perhaps. The carp gawped, opening the maiden's mouth and sunk its flesh into a cleverly disguised hook. In shock, it froze, and was soon reeled up and wrangled from the maiden's body, which surfaced a few moments later, gasping for breath. The fisherman, forgetting about his catch, dropped the carp onto the sand, where it unsuccessfully writhed for water. The fisherman pulled the maiden from the water and took her to his cottage, where he fed and clothed her, and eventually asked her to live with him as his wife, an offer she happily accepted.

Still every evening, just as before, she could not sleep. She could not breathe because she did not know how to fill all the space inside her chest. She often thought of the carp which they had left to rot on the loamy lakeside sand. The hollow chamber inside her chest ached and seemed to expand under her heightened awareness of it. Sometimes she thought she heard the carp's nagging, felt its disapproving twitch within her frame, but when she put her hands to her chest, it felt vast and quiet, like open ocean. As gray and empty as a broken-down lighthouse, she'd stand watching her husband by the lake. At night she would not let him touch her chest or rub her back, although he dearly longed to. If he ever woke to find her uncovered, he'd pull the covers up to her neck, just like he'd swaddled her in wool the day he'd rescued her. After he'd fallen back asleep, she'd pull them off again, re-exposing her skin to the cold.

In dreams the carp urged her to rescue its skeleton. *Provide me a home as fine as the one I gave you*, it said. Unable to refuse the voice anymore, the maiden quietly ran to search for the carp's bones in the moonlight. She thrashed through the sand, digging, and finally found them glistening in the grass, as if someone had cleaned and polished them for her. The maiden cradled them to her empty chest, squeezing the bones sharply against her flesh. Her husband found her like that later, lying in the grass with bones shoved in her mouth, some piercing her breasts like tiny spears, and a fish skull nestled wetly in her throat.

Bedtime with Frummy's Friend

by AJD

Note: This story uses the non-gender pronouns e / em / eirs and they / them / theirs for some characters.

"There once was a monster who lived under the bed. The monster stayed there, and slept mostly, until hungry. Then the monster ate the child who slept above, and went away, to a different bed.

"The monster ate a new child every eleven-point-six days, on average.

"The monster could go anywhere in all of time and all of space. Anywhere there were beds, and anytime there were children to eat -- though that was mostly around three-forty-seven-a-m, statistically speaking.

"But that could be any day, any month, or any year, ever.

"And it could be on any one of the thirty-two planets and four-hundred-and-fifty-three planetoids that our species eventually ends up inhabiting, before the...

"Well... No sense in getting ahead of ourselves.

"So, that's how the monster ended up under your bed, and that's why I'm telling you this, to prepare you to meet the monster, to be eaten all."

"Ahh-hh," the child interrupted.

"Ha! Just kidding. Har de har. Wanted to make sure you're still listening."

"Who, who are you?" The child pulled up a handful of blankets, protectively.

"Oh, silly. Don'choo 'member? We were all out in the other room. I'm your frummy's friend. Frummy told me to tuck you in and tell you all about how there are no monsters under the bed, or anything like that."

"But, but, that's not what you said. You—"

"Might as well," Frummy's friend leaned over to the small table and retrieved an ornate drinking glass, a large goblet. "The monster's not around anymore anyway."

"Why?" The child bolted upright in bed. "Why, huh, why? 'Cause you said the monster could come in anytime! YOU—"

"Now, now. Just sit back and listen to the story, whydon'cha? Here's how it happened, how it will happen, and how it is happening now," Frummy's friend attempted to lean back into the rocking chair, but was hindered by narrowing arms on the child-sized furniture.

"Oh, brother..." said the child, accompanied by an epic eye roll.

"Shush." Frummy's friend drank, leaned forward, and belched softly before continuing. "Now, someplace and sometime -- not here -- the monster was under a bed and decided it was time for supper.

"The house was all quiet, except for the small struggle on top of the bed, where the meal was having a bad dream. The monster waited for times like these, the best -- the absolute best -- time to eat a child. All the monster cookbooks say so."

"I don't like this story."

"Shush. Frummy says you have to listen."

"Really?"

"Really. So, the monster extracted this quite delicious brain juice, after a great many intricate preparations. This was quite valuable."

"Did Frummy really?"

"Yes," Frummy's friend drank deeply from the goblet, then peered over the rim and waited for another interruption. The child stayed silent.

"So, besides the feasting, the monster was laying in stores, for the future." The goblet descended into Frummy's friend's lap. "Oh, but the feasting, that would last some two or three days, according to our time. The preparation and preserving for the stores, there was a bit of that, of course. But mostly it was feasting. Then a big, long, happy, sleep."

While listening, the child had retreated into the bed, rearranging the pillows, plush toys, the special quilts and coverings, and finally pulling hands and arms beneath the innermost sheet. Frummy's friend did not react to the child's attempted camouflage.

"Since the monster could go anywhere and anytime there were beds and children, it just slipped out of whatever here/now it was projecting into when it all began. Just like that."

Frummy's friend raised their hands to either side of their head, the drink tilted, threatening to spill. "Poof! You're gone. They're gone, rather." The hands and cup back down, temporarily.

"The monster and its meal almost always reappear in an alcove universe -- one which most experts now agree it creates for this very purpose -- usually within the property of a snug, split-level ranch house, in the middle of a lava flow. It has a large indoor-outdoor kitchen and patio area, with a wonderful view and sulfur breeze, where it spends most of its waking hours.

"Oh, yes. Good times. Um, I'd imagine so, anyway." Frummy's friend stared down towards the remaining beverage swirling in the bottom of the drinking vessel, glancing up on the fourth rotation. "Well, don't you have anything to say?"

"So..." the child responded from inside a short tunnel of plush, "Who cares? The monster's still eating the, meal. I mean, you're—"

"Shush," Frummy's friend waved dismissively. "You're being silly again. Frummy said you're afraid of the monster under the bed, so I'm explaining how "

"Not helping."

"You haven't heard it all. It gets better and worse, round and round. You never know who's eating who half the time." Frummy's friend drained their goblet and set it on the table, then turned back towards the bed and waited, head cocked.

After a long pause, a tiny voice said, "Fine." The child pulled a heavy quilt upwards, past eir nose, then spoke louder so eir muffled voice could be heard. "Go ahead, but I'm calling Frummy if it gets weird. Too weird."

"Sure, but Frummy is tired. And you are too…" They looked around absently, then jerked around, up, and out of the chair. "Now, Frummy's friend will be right back."

They stumbled into a shaft of dim blue light and white noise from the other room and returned the same way, but carrying a jug and a large piece of cake.

"All right, now." They set the cake on the far edge of the table, then filled the goblet and set the jug on the floor against the wall.

"Gently, the monster slithered out from under the bed. The child above, tensing and loosening, struggling to scream in the nightmare climax of your -- its, I mean, their -- subconscious mind."

They tore off a piece of cake, chewed, and swallowed.

"It stole quietly from under the bed and approached its meal. First one tentacle, then the—"

"Stay over there," the child warned in a wooly voice.

"I am. It's just a story, you know. And the world is not like that -- all the experts say."

"I know. It's just not..." The child pulled down the quilt below eir chin to be better heard. "Not helping me to sleep, for one thing. And—"

"You sound sleepy already, to me. Anyway, let's just turn down the lights. Which is your night-light? We'll leave that one on."

"No. NO!" Upright again, the child gestured wide, indicating the entirety of the cramped bedroom. "Leave them ALL on. Frummy does that. After I go to sleep, she leaves. And she leaves on this one, ON, here, on the bookshelf, and maybe another. The others, some of them -- a few of them -- can go off. You do that."

"Okay. Don't worry about it. Jeesh. Can I just turn off a few of the lights, now? I only need the one, right here on the table."

"No."

"Ah, c'mon. Frummy's friend doesn't like all this light in their eyes, not at all."

"Well, you can turn off that one, there."

"Thanks." Frummy's friend leaned forward and switched off the tricolored disco spinner.

"You see, anyway, it doesn't matter to the monster if all the lights are on, or not. So you might as well leave them off, as far as getting eaten is concerned. Up to you, though."

Frummy's friend took another drink as the child settled back beneath the layers. "Where was I? Oh, yes...

"Hook and tentacle up the side of the bed. The child twitches weakly, desperate to let loose the silent scream strangled in its throat," Frummy's friend rocked back and forth, hamming it up, "unable to thrash out into the waking world it senses all around."

"In the nightmare world, the monster's giant head rears into view. It blocks the wall, the lights of the dream bedroom. Its open mouth looms, bigger and bigger, closer and closer.

"You see inside. You see everything. And you feel wonderful. Ecstatic.

"Inside the mouth -- tiny dolphins and sea otters and apple trees and jungle gyms, all attached to the sides and roof of the mouth, extending far back and down, into the throat, all dancing -- little pink nodes, aware, part of the cosmic cycle and happy in their manifestation.

"Everyone participating, as matter is swapped back and forth, back and forth.

"The happy, swaying dance lures you in and you realize what it is ALL about. Finally. You peer into the abyss, a whirring cycle where you merge and you reemerge.

"Where you are remembered and reappear.

"The tongue, a warm, wet carpet slide down a familiar stairwell, while a seed of gnosis sprouts to reveal wider worlds -- plural, have you -- all around. You learn to step through dimensions and can continue on any timeline you want. There is death and there is transcendence.

"There is choice.

"Most, of course, pass through unknowing." Slurp. Click. "They close their eyes for the journey. Once that decision is made, to close one's eyes, the passage can be swift. So, for those in, uh, that there/then, there is no remembering. Their pasts are lost to them. They are onto something new, for better or worse.

"But, you see, the monster offers its meals so much more.

"If only they are brave enough to realize, to accept.

"To become the meal that sees." Click.

"Now -- and always -- the terrible price of this world... That's always there. Always. This is the predominant view, anyway, especially at moments like this.

"That's what most folk would dwell on here, I mean there.

"But there -- and here -- there is so much more." Chew, chew, gulp. "Imagine, the meal dodging into the near/then, or subsuming entirely to reappear elsewhen. To change its contingeries -- the particuwots and whositarries -- at its whim. At its peck and caw, if you will.

"If it chooses."

Shuffle, shuffle, shuffle. Gurgle, gurgle, gulp, gulp, gurgle, gurgle. Frummy's friend repositioned the jug and sat back down in the rocker. "Sadly, it can only gain this knowledge at a certain price." Chew, gulp.

The child moaned, nearly asleep, and turned to face the wall, away from the storyteller. Instantly, even beneath the layers, e felt eir back raw and exposed. E jumped back in one dramatic hop, the blanket fortress barely moving.

"Now, don'choo worry about me." Frummy's friend started up from the chair. The goblet went to the table, mashing cake and icing into the patterned cloth. "You should just close your eyes again. That's the whole point of this exercise. To send you off into the subconscious. Aware, and forewarned, but still... Off to Oz you must go, and see it for—"

"...oh, brother," the child whispered, pulling the entire blanket terrain a few inches while turning slightly to the side.

"Always the critic, this one. Anyway, I think I might have -- perhaps -- become, a bit -- a bit, I'll have you -- sidefracked there. So, let me pick it up again, properly.

"Have you ever seen a frog eat a large insect? No?

"Well, something like that will be the end result, of course, though the monster will first proceed with its extractions. So let's get those tiresome details out of the way.

"And, before any of that, the ceremonies, the oblations, the recognition, the blessings, the story. Blah, blah. It's always a different path but the same journey.

"Where and when it ends..." Click. "Well, that will be up to you, the meal I mean.

"And let's get this out in the open. Clear the air, if you will. It may have crossed your mind: oh no, you won't be YOU, then, after all this.

"'I won't be ME, waa!'

"Well, you're only you for right now, and not a second longer. You're always something new, different, and always were.

"When you close your eyes here and open them again down there, you're in the underworld, where all things are made and unmade. You can come out the other side again, of course, if that's what you want." Slurp. "Something always does, anyway.

"It's up to you. If you want to continue.

"It's easy, peasy. A dream, really. Once you decide to see.

"And, more basically, IF you decide to see. Because, if you see, you will eventually understand. And that is good, because you will need to know several terrible truths if you want to navigate your dreams with any confidence.

"And you must be careful. Despite the possibility and promise of all this jumping around, nothing is safe. If you choose to look, to see through the veil, and so acquire the possibility to travel at your will through worlds...

"Well, you need to first know this: there is only one of you. Only one you. Only one.

"Just like the monster.

"And that is a beautiful and awful thing."

Slurp.

"Especially in the somewhen where digestive acids are hard at work."

Gulp.

***

The child twisted and moaned inside a narrow pool of warm color, which radiated outward from a sun night-light clipped nearby. The reddish crown dipped into dark penumbra at the edges of the small bed.

The child had started to fall, accelerating through the night air, precipitating an abrupt end to the dreamscape. Reaching upward from the nightmare, e bumped the bookshelf, knocking loose the bulb, which flickered off.

The child peered up at the dark board and the shadow-laced ceiling beyond. The knot in eir stomach from the dream fall loosened. E moved aside the pillows and stuffed animals, then crept outward, into view.

There was just one light source inside the room now, a blue-green fish, sparkling above the toy chest in the corner. The bed was as dark as it ever had been, when the child was there. E didn't know about other times.

A pale light from the other room fell into a slanted rectangle on the wood floor. The child got out of the bed, dipped into slippers, and slipped into what Frummy called the living room. Sinking into the thickly padded carpeting of the larger room, e felt a sense of vertigo. Then everything seemed to be underwater for a moment.

E approached a battery-operated lamp perched precariously atop a nearby fruit crate, carefully turning the big dial on top. The light was yellowish-white at the very bottom, then orange-red above, as filtered through a taped-on plastic shade. This commingled with the emanations of a blue-white rectangular screen, beaming down from a high ledge near the front door, some ten feet away.

The child navigated the cluttered area between the coffee table and the couch, then gently pulled and tugged at the macramé throw so it better covered Frummy. Retreating from Frummy's harbor, e ventured across the sea of thick pile carpet. At the ragged edge of the room, e stopped, the tips of eir slippers brushing the border to the kitchen's cracked red linoleum.

Despite badly craving cake, e hesitated, concerned at the darkness in the far end, towards the utility room and the head. Normally, a light in the corner of the hallway provided a reliable guide to the back part of the apartment.

It was off, or out. E stared into the dim recesses there for some time.

Eventually, the child stepped into the kitchen, climbed atop a chair, and pulled steadily down on a twine cord above the small table. A fluorescent circle buzzed to life and lit everything through a bug-encrusted dome of frosted glass. E swayed back and forth atop the chair, examining the larger of the dead moths, then clambered down to the scarred flooring.

E searched all the exposed surfaces -- counters, tables, cutting board, even back out to the coffee table and fruit crate -- nothing. E turned off the buggy kitchen light, since Frummy didn't like it on when she stirred, and could wake up mad and difficult.

With only the two small lights from the living room as beacons, e stepped toward the fridge, a solid monolith of quiet power with its own cycle of purring and shuddering. A crayon drawing of a raven was impaled to its middle by a black circle magnet.

The child swung open the metal door and was drenched in the cold, greenish light. Plates of raw meat, condensation dripping from the plastic wrapping and pooling in pink puddles below, occupied two glass shelves. E searched every bright compartment -- all of which went dark when no one was looking -- but still no cake.

E stared at one of the meat packages, drawn to the little tubes of pink and white, curled around one another. E thought about the talking farm animals from storybooks.

There was a faint scratching in the hall and the child stood stock still, then turned ever so slightly to peer past the fridge.

There was still nothing out of place in the hallway. Nothing that e could see.

But what about the utility room? And where was Frummy's friend?

The child was thinking about the door latch -- hoping it was firmly closed, in case there was some kind of creature back there, with all their old stuff and stores and boxes -- when the screen in the living room went to sleep.

The kitchen side of the apartment darkened a bit -- but the other side of the apartment transformed into a soft dim blur, illuminated only by weak lamplight.

Before the refrigerator door had swung shut, the child darted across the room, switched off the orange lamp, and stood in the doorway to the fish-lit bedroom.

As the green and pink light from the kitchen narrowed to nothing, e checked to make sure that the whoosh-thunk-clink sound of the refrigerator door shutting did not wake Frummy, then jumped to bed in three big leaps. With eyes closed, the child thought of cake, but saw shelves of meat.

The End

The Garden of W's Beginning

by Andy Anderson

On the east side of town lived a human. This being was neither male nor female nor was this being sure where ze came from. No god was present to tell zir that ze came from dust, therefore the being, who was named W, assumed ze came from the water. All ze ever knew was the water. It came from below and was all around. W also knew ze had breath and therefore, ze was alive.

W, who lived in the east, had a garden. In the garden were many trees and also ground shrubbery, which bore fruit in season. Leafy greens, tall beans, wispy sprouts, and juicy round red spheres were abounding. Everything grew plentiful because of the water that was all around. W and zir garden drank the water and grew fruitful and happy.

The water, which took the form of a river, continued on beyond the east. The flow gave formation to the gold in the hills, and the black onyx underground. The water also gave life to the farther lands, the names of which W did not know. Ze simply knew that the river did not belong to zir, but to the ground from which it sprung.

One tree in W's garden was a lilac tree. Ze named it so because of the flowers that bloomed only briefly as the weather warmed. It wasn't poisonous, but simply bland and W would rather simply honor it for its beauty. W sat under the tree often and pondered zir small existence. W called the garden zirs and ze was happy and unafraid. The beauty, the nourishment, and life all around W were enough.

W passed the time by giving names to the creatures nearby. W named one furry creature Mittens, after the blue fur that covered its paws. Ze named the fish a school, and the cows, cattle [after zir favorite creature by far, the cat]. Ze called the flying creatures with feathers a flock and the small white fluttery one a foth.

W often fell into naming trances by the diversity around, and never found one quite as unique as zirself.

During one fitful dream, W was overcome with cramps high in the ribcage, short breath, and the heat of the night. Ze was having a wild dream wrought with intense dehydration of the land and of zir body. Ze woke up lost, panicked, and barren. Shortly after, W realized that ze was no longer alone.

"You were having a nightmare" spoke a voice standing above.

W sat up suddenly, pondered then repeated the word "nightmare." Ze was immediately lost in the purple eyes of this human being standing in front of zir.

"Lilac. I shall call you Lilac."

W couldn't help but name the being; after all it was all ze knew to do. W was also overcome with happiness beyond zir fruitful garden, for this being looked so similar to zir reflection in the water. W thought Lilac was magical.

Lilac loved the garden of W's beginning and loved all the creatures ze named, and all the ones ze didn't. W and Lilac drank the water and together they lived and they were happy and unafraid.

Lilac came especially to love the lilac tree but was frustrated anytime it wasn't in bloom. She ached to see the flowers that she was named after.

One day, while W was away, one of the garden cats sauntered over, climbed the lilac tree, and chomped on one of the drooping leaves. Lilac, the being, was shocked at the feline's audacity. She had never eaten from the lilac, not from the leaves, nor from its grape-like flowers. But that brave and sweltering day, she too picked some of the leaves out of boredom, curiosity (and a bit in spite of its lack of flowers) and made use of the lilac tree, as the cat had done. Lilac, the newest being to the garden made a full meal of the leaves, and upon W's return, they all ate together, the cats and the human beings.

Only when their bowls were empty, and the sky darkened, did W bring the news of zir travels,

"My nightmare? It is true, the fires… they are spreading. The drought has intensified."

They realized immediately that the sun caused this bad news, not their odd meal. None of this was their fault but regardless their eyes were opened and they knew that preparations should be made. A summer like none other was coming.

Right away, they began to sew together lilac leaves (and other green leaves) to keep their being skin safe from the sun and the magnified light.

They argued as the river dried up and soil became tough. Life was much, much harder. Again, this was not for any reason but that the sun burned brighter this unfortunate year, the fires were spreading and happiness wasn't as plentiful.

The wind carried death & change and Lilac & W were very afraid.

So with sadness in their hearts, Lilac & W made love one last time under the lilac tree. Then, they took each other in their arms & said we must move farther east where vegetables grow year round and the rain falls in heaps and where they could be naked once again.

Yes, they were afraid but they knew together they were knowledgeable enough to build again.

And so, that is the end of W's beginning.

Together, Lilac & W, who now preferred the name "Wanderer," along with their devoted cats, left the garden and never looked back. They continued on past the hills of gold and onyx until together they found water in the land with no name and then again, they were unafraid.

It was good that they never looked back, for the garden was ablaze and an unnamed creature stood guard. Was it a Minotaur? They would never know.

Loosely based off of heresay, but also Genesis 2:8- Genesis 3:24, so mostly heresy.

Interview with Sarah Nicole Donaldson

Deep Overstock (DO): In your paper "The Secret Life of the Cross-Cultural Fairy Tale," you argue that a heroine's agency is diminished when she is robbed of her wealth. Why study the transaction of money in fairy tales?

Sarah Donaldson (SD): The acquisition of wealth is a common goal for characters in fairy tales. Heroes go on adventures to seek jewels. Kings marry maidens who are gifted with the ability to produce gold. Until I began this comparative study, I hadn't realized just how pervasive an element it is in fairy tales.

DO: In "Breaking Down the Women's Sphere," you note the subjugation of women to the domestic sphere portrayed in and reinforced by Indonesian media created during the New Order regime of Suharto's presidency (1966-1998), and the regime had a heavy hand in the production of this media. You cite the film Pasir Berbisik (2001) as a strong feminist film. How does it use folklore? And is this folklore used to uphold subjugation, to criticize it, or to dismantle it?

SD: First I will provide a brief synopsis of the plot. At the beginning of the film, Berlian and her daughter, Daya, live alone in a village in East Java. We learn that Agus, Berlian's husband and Daya's father, had left them when Daya was still a child. After Berlian and Daya flee their village during the anti-communist massacre of 1965-66, Agus returns. For a short time they live happily as a family. Then, one day, Agus sells Daya as a prostitute. When Berlian finds out what Agus has done, she poisons him. By the end of the film, Berlian tells Daya to go out on her own, stating, "There's nothing left anymore."

At the beginning, we see Daya play with the shadow puppets her father, a puppeteer, had left behind. Later in the film, she is given a mask by a man she meets during her travels. The man tells her to wear the mask on the back of her head so "the ghost of the desert cannot bring [her] underground."

It is important to note here that shadow puppet theater, traditionally performed by men, is used to recount war epics. In my paper, I argue that the female leads adopt this traditionally masculine performance of violence as a survival tactic in war-torn Indonesia. During the murder scene, in particular, Berlian embodies a shadow puppet. Her positioning within the foreground of the frame exaggerates her largeness of presence, while Agus sits behind her. (During a performance of shadow puppet theater, the performer holds the "murdering" puppet farther from the screen, thus enlarging its silhouette on the screen.) Furthermore, much of Berlian's face is concealed by shadow.

As for the mask? I believe it represents the omnipresent mother, who seems to, as the mask-giver says, have "eyes on the back of her head." Innocent and naive, Daya lacks this awareness of her surroundings. Throughout the film, she is wholly dependent upon her mother.

DO: You use fairy tale-like monsters in your own fiction. What do you think makes a good monster?

SD: One that possesses the ability to use your own strengths against you.

DO: What is your favorite Indonesian folklore?

SD: Anything that makes me laugh. I love ketoprak, which is a form of improv theater. In the city of Surabaya, I once watched a performance of ketoprak in which an actor tried to "stab" another actor (costumed as a tiger) with the sheath of his sword. The tiger fainted, but the man couldn't drag the tiger offstage. Finally, the man shook the tiger awake and rode him offstage. I'll leave it to the Freudians among you to analyze that one.

.   .   .   .

Read the rest of this interview on deepoverstock.com.

Fairy Tales with Coleman Stevenson and Ariel Kusby

Ariel Kusby (AK): Hi! Let's talk about fairy tales!

Coleman Stevenson (CS): Yes!

AK: You are a poet, writer, visual artist, and tarot deck designer. Tell me a little bit about how your work is informed by fairy tales, folklore, and archetypes?

CS: I think my work is influenced by these in so many ways, from surface content to subtle undercurrents, to structural design. For example, I sometimes compose poems that overtly take a particular tale as subject, but I know that I am also so deeply infused with these stories and symbols they are pouring out of me all the time whether intended or not. I also am a fan of patterning, probably due in part to my early absorption of fairy tales and the years I spent in structuralist analysis of folk narrative (a delight to me but probably torture for my students when I'd make them memorize Olrik's "Epic Laws of Folk Narrative"). As an artist now, I often conceive of the structure of a book, deck, or visual series before much specific content is even decided. I love systems. Just like an archaeologist or a botanist, there's a real joy in discovering what a found specimen is, and in analyzing how structure and meaning are unified.

It's also important to me to make archetypal ideas accessible to people, so I have been exploring characters from tarot narratives in multisensory ways, in particular attempting to translate something of their essences into wearable scents. I'm also beginning a new line of scents inspired by famous paintings. Maybe I should make some for fairy tale characters as well…

AK: A line of scents based on fairy tales would be so awesome! I love the idea that archetypes can be multifaceted and multisensory. In what ways can you examine archetypes more deeply through hybrid art forms than through traditional storytelling?

CS: There's something about keeping it from being too fixed to the page… When these stories were exclusively oral, they had such a life of their own, altered subtly by transmission. So delivering the content now in a multifaceted way seems to liberate it again.

AK: I like the idea of freeing or liberating an archetype. In what ways do you think these structures hold us hostage? And in what ways have we constrained them? If it's impossible to not retell these classic stories, how much free will do we actually have as storytellers?

CS: Well, to answer this best I have to state that I am an absolute believer that these stories have always been used for enculturation, indoctrination, or control. Initially, of course, this was an informal education in how to survive in a particular culture. Later the stories were locked down, moralized, and intentionally used to teach children how to behave in the way a certain society deemed appropriate. Because of print, as societies changed, the stories didn't. The same literary versions are still accessible and read today because of print, but they are divorced from the social situations that crafted them. Even though their messages are outdated, we keep delivering them.

That said, we have long been revising and updating them in various media as well. For example, we retell them with a feminist slant, or place them in contemporary contexts which require certain content to be swapped out for something modern, for which there may or may not be an equivalent. When the context shifts, so does the message.

With all our media we have the ability to maintain or to shift societal norms. We tell the same stories, but perhaps we can think more about shifting the characters and breaking other expectations of plot and outcomes.

AK: You mentioned feeling so infused with folkloric stories and archetypes that they come out in your work whether you are conscious of it or not. Why do you think this is? Disney? The collective unconscious? How you were raised? A mixture of all of these?

CS: It's a mixture of these, for sure. We've largely replaced oral storytelling in our general culture by new media. Fairy tales are read verbatim out of books, or watched as cartoons. They are also knowingly adapted and modernized in film, literature, advertising, and product design. But the tale types and motifs are so long a part of our lives from times of oral telling through today that we are often defaulting to them even when we think we are composing a new narrative.

AK: In what ways are you interested in making fairy tales new/ contemporary? Or is this even possible?

CS: We as writers and artists may not realize the underlying origins of some of the stories we tell, but those frames and mo- tifs are there all the same. Since it's impossible to not constantly borrow, rehash, adapt, I think I am most interested in having the use be overt, intentionally drawing parallels between certain stories and characters and the occurrences of my own life. I like hiding personal information in poems inside elements from classic tales.

AK: Did you have a favorite fairy tale as a child?

CS: I know that a Grimm collection was in regular rotation at bedtime, but I have trouble differentiating certain tales orally conveyed to me then from their Disney film versions, also watched then. Stand-out stories from early childhood are "Sleeping Beauty" and "Cinderella." "Sleeping Beauty" had a strange elegance about it, some kind of aspiration quality which now seems horrifying to me. With "Cinderella," I remember being filled with dread for her (and fear for myself ever being in such a position), and then anticipation to see that everything would work out ok in the end.

.   .   .   .

Read the rest of this interview on deepoverstock.com.

Bios

AJD
AJD is a bookseller who has also worked as a writer, among other things.

Andy Anderson
With a mix of authentic vulnerability, relevant truth, and humor, Andy Anderson writes poems that immediately make you want to be their friend. They are a co-organizer of Byrony Blaze's Queer Poetry Takeover in Portland, OR.

Jaya Blackburn
Jaya is fascinated with books, writing and putting words together to create experience. Favorite themes include death, spirituality and fantasy realms. Jaya has a minor in writing from PSU and is about to start working on her masters in thanatology – the study of death and dying. Jaya just celebrated her very first publication in an anthology independently published in PDX by Arq Press. When she dies she wants her ashes spread in the poetry section of Powell's Books.

Katie Borak
Born in northern New Jersey, Katie Borak escaped as quickly as she could. She can be found in Portland, OR pursuing an MFA in the PSU Creative Writing program, facilitating free creative writing workshops for underserved communities with Write Around Portland, or at Powell's Books hawking children's Bibles and barbecue cookbooks.

Michael Calkins
Michael Calkins has worked in bookstores for 31 years, the last 28 at Powell's. This is his first published story.

Mickey Collins
~~Mickey rights wrongs. Mickey wrongs rites.~~ Mickey writes words, sometimes wrong words but he tries to get it write.

Sarah Nicole Donaldson
Sarah is a writer, folklorist, and filmmaker. Her short documentary film on the multiracial identity, "What Are You?," was aired on Oregon Public Broadcast in 2015. She has presented her research at national academic conferences, and is currently working on a middle grade fantasy series based on Indonesian folklore. She splits her time between Portland, Oregon

and Surabaya, East Java. Prior to her writing career, Sarah worked in the Reserves section of the Portland State University Library.

ROBERT EVERSMANN
bb was a bookseller at Powell's City of Books. They have specialized in aviation, philosophy, biology and Judaism in Purple, Red and Pearl rooms. But their heart is with the Rose room because it is a constant storm of book throwing and because kids books are the coolest. bb is a developmental editor, specializing in literary novels, YA and MG novels, realistic, science fiction, romance and fantasy. Their work is in Portland Review, Fiction Southwest, fog machine and SUSAN/The Journal. Their website is roberteversmann.com.

JOE GALVÁN
Joe Galván has always written and sold his own books, but for two years in his junior and senior years of college, he sold textbooks at a small bookstore in Lubbock, Texas. A writer and reader since childhood, he has just finished a novel and is working on a series of zines on manners and etiquette for millennials. He can be reached on Twitter @fadopapi.

DAN HEISE
Dan Heise is an actor and writer who works at Powell's City of Books part time. He enjoys reading plays and young adult novels, and enjoys writing poems and plays. He often can't decide whether he likes puns or Lord of the Rings more.

ULA JANKOWSKA
Ula Jankowska, in some cities known as Miss Bookseller, is interested in books and people. Never leaves home without at least three books in her bag. Used to work as a bookseller for around 14 years now, in Warsaw, Wroclaw and Cracow. Now she is starting her own bookshop project in Prague. If you ask her to name three favourite writers, she will still name more and between these names will show up Italo Calvino, Jorge Louis Borges, Bohumil Hrabal, Ota Pavel, Tove Jansson.

SARA KACHELMAN
Sara Kachelman's work has appeared in *DIAGRAM*, *Fanzine*, and *Portland Review*. She lives in a basement.

ARIEL KUSBY
Ariel Kusby is a writer and bookseller based in Portland, Oregon. She currently works in the Rose and Orange rooms at Powell's City of Books, where she pays special attention to children's books about witches, odd

cookbooks, and gnome gardening guides. You can check out her writing at
www.arielkusby.com.

EMILY LAKEHOMER
Emily is an Aries sun, Cancer moon, and Virgo rising. She works at Powell's.

KELLYE MCBRIDE
Kellye McBride lives in Portland with her dog, Pucci. When she's not writing
flash fiction, she works as a copyeditor for science and technical books. In
a former life, she shelved books at a library and told fortunes before being
burned at the stake.

MAYA MCOMIE
Maya is a poet, performer and daydreamer who probably spends too much
time thinking about snacks. She grew up with two languages and cultures
and her poetry and art attempts to process the complex emotions that are
part of being a person. She works in a bookstore where, to much joy and
chagrin, she finds at least ten things she wants to read every day.

TIMOTHY MERRITT
Timothy Merritt is a writer and musician who wakes up each day during
the witching hour to put words to paper. He's previously been published
in Alchemy and Alembic, the literary journals of Portland Community
College, and has presented at the Northwest Undergraduate Conference on
Literature. He holds a B.A. in English from Marylhurst University, where he
was the recipient of the Binford Writing Scholarship. When he's not drafting
tales of the weird and surreal, he can usually be found working among the
aisles of Powell's City of Books. He lives in Portland, Oregon with his wife
and children.

AZALEA MICKETTI
Azalea Micketti is a writer, director, and bookseller who is passionate about
storytelling and sharing books. She grew up in Ashland, OR and has lived in
her (second) favorite city for almost nine months. She works at Powell's City
of Books on the Inventory Team.

OAKTEA
Oaktea has always been in love with every aspect of a book--from the design
to its contents, everything contributes to the experience. She started making
comics for the all-in-one art and words combination, and eventually started
working in bookstores to feed her voracious habit, as well as her love and
respect for the form of the book itself.

Olivia Olivia

Olivia Olivia's writing has appeared in *Salon, The Rumpus, The Establishment, Ex-Berliner,* and the *Portland Mercury,* among other places. Her speculative memoir set in the afterlife, NO ONE REMEMBERED YOUR NAME BUT I WROTE IT DOWN, is available through Impossible Wings Press. Prepare yourselves. You can follow her work at OLIVIAWRITES.COM, on FACEBOOK, and on TWITTER.

Piers Rippey

Piers Rippey is all about dogs these days. He draws dogs, thinks about dogs, walks dogs. He is a bookseller at Powell's City of Books where he helps run the Purple, Red and Pearl rooms.

Phoenix Singer

Phoenix Singer is a writer and theorist based in Portland. Their writing has appeared on Queen Mobs and The Establishment, and they are currently editing a Gender Nihilist anthology. Submit your thoughts and manifestos to gendernihilistjouranl@gmail.com.

Coleman Stevenson

Coleman Stevenson is an illustrator, writer and tarot practitioner based in Portland, OR. She is the artist behind the Dark Exact Tarot Deck and the author of *Breakfast: 43 Poems* (Reprobate/GobQ Books, 2015) and *The Accidental Rarefication of Pattern #5609* (bedouin books, 2012). Her poems have appeared in a variety of publications such as *Paper Darts, Seattle Review, Gramma, E-ratio, Louisiana Literature,* and *Mid-American Review.* She has taught at a number of Portland institutions in subjects including poetry writing, literature, curation & interaction, folklore, culture & design, and image & text interplay.

Robert Torres

Robert Torres is a local writer and actor. Their work explores the changeable nature of reality and the trouble of having a body whether you like it or not. They have been featured locally at Á Reading, Salon Skid Row, and elsewhere. They have appeared on stage with Monkey with a Hat on.

Jonathan van Belle

Jonathan van Belle is a bookseller at Powell's. He's the author of three books, including the pre-posthumously published *Charter Party Companion to Private Holidays* (all available in the most spider-infested kudzu undergrowth of Amazon). At the moment, Jonathan is working to build a philosophical community in Portland, with the aim of establishing a permanent residence for the *Portland Philosophy Museum.*

www.ingramcontent.com/pod-product-compliance
Lightning Source LLC
Chambersburg PA
CBHW032018180726
48283CB00008B/2738